Laura felt herself being hoisted from the ground and dragged backwards towards the statue. "Hey! Let me go!" she shouted, twisting her head form side to side and struggling for all she was worth.

Two men wearing camouflage uniforms gripped her arms tightly and did their best to avoid her flailing feet. Another man, dressed all in black, his bespectacled face twitching angrily, stood in the cavern shouting instructions at the guards.

"Prince!" screamed Laura desperately. "Fetch! Fetch Jack! Fetch Peggy! GO!"

As Prince took to his heels, she was dragged, kicking and screaming, through the entrance into a neon-lit tunnel. The wings of the statue closed and the cavern was silent once more.

Other titles available
in this series:

1. The Secret Island
2. The Secret of Spiggy Holes
4. The Secret of Moon Castle
5. The Secret Mountain

Enid Blyton's™

THE SECRET
OF KILLIMOOIN

Screenplay novelisation
by Helen Wire

Collins
An imprint of HarperCollinsPublishers

For further information on Enid Blyton™ please contact
www.blyton.com

Original screenplay by Charles Hodges

This screenplay novelisation first published in
Great Britain by Collins 1998
Collins is an imprint of HarperCollins*Publishers* Ltd
77-85 Fulham Palace Road, Hammersmith,
London, W6 8JB

1 3 5 7 9 8 6 4 2

Copyright © Enid Blyton Ltd 1998.
All rights reserved. Developed from the TV script
which is © Cloud 9 Screen Entertainment.

ISBN 0 00 675316-7

Enid Blyton's signature mark and
Mystery & Adventure are trademarks of
Enid Blyton Ltd.

Printed and bound in Great Britain by
Caledonian International Book Manufacturing Ltd,
Glasgow G64

CHAPTER ONE

"What else does Paul say, Ruby?" asked Jack, leaning forward eagerly. He and his friends were poring over a large map whilst the Arnold children's nanny, Ruby, read out a letter from their friend, Prince Paul of Baronia.

Peggy and the twins, Mike and Laura, sprawled comfortably round Ruby with their honey-coloured collie, Prince, beside them. Prince's ears were cocked as if he wanted to hear the news too! Peggy was tracking her index finger across the map.

"Well," said Ruby in surprise, "Paul says there's something we have to do when we meet the King. Listen to this:

> *When presented to my father, His Majesty the King of Baronia, adults must kneel before him, remove one of his shoes and throw it over their shoulder. Then they must announce with the utmost dignity, "The King's feet go everywhere!"*

"What?" spluttered all four children, roaring with laughter.

"I think they're a bit weird in Baronia," groaned Ruby, peering at them over the top of the letter.

"Hey! I've found the King's lodge where we'll be staying. Look, here, on the north side of Killimooin Mountains!" exclaimed Peggy. They all looked at where she was pointing as she added, "And here's the Secret Forest Paul told us about."

"Wow! This is going to be a great holiday! I hope Dad gets here in time to take us to the airport! I'm longing to see the wilds of Baronia. It's going to be fantastic!" said Laura breathlessly.

"Good heavens!" gasped Ruby, looking at her watch, "We'd better get a move on or we won't be going out of the door, let alone to Baronia. I hope your dad's lecture was so brilliant the audience haven't needed to hold him up with a zillion questions about that old Devil Spider. But if Thaddeus is running late, we'd better be ready to leave the instant he gets here. So, hop to it, you lot. Get packing!"

Charlotte Clancy clapped heartily as her friend Thaddeus Arnold – the children's father – came into the lecture hall to give his speech to the Worldwide Nature Association. She took a quick photograph of him as he neared the centre of the stage, but she could see he was far too nervous even to look her way.

Charlotte also took a photo of the spotlit object on a table beside the speaker's lectern. Not much larger than a shoebox, it was covered with a dark cloth. In it was the famous Maluku Devil Spider. Then her attention was drawn back to Thaddeus – he was about to begin.

Thaddeus glanced at the box, drew a deep breath and faced the audience. "Until recently, I thought there was little left on this planet that could still surprise me," he said, gazing about the room. "But that was before I visited the tropical forests of Maluku. It was there I saw a creature many people believed to be extinct."

He paused, considering his words carefully.

"It has been my enormous good fortune and great privilege to have captured one of these rare specimens. And also, upon my return with it to this country, to be entrusted with its study, and care."

He self-consciously straightened his tie and stepped over to the table. Pinching the dark cloth between his thumb and forefinger, he continued, "Ladies and gentlemen, I give you… the Maluku Devil Spider!"

With a flourish, Thaddeus whipped off the

cover. He stepped back to allow the spotlight to fall dramatically on a transparent box. There, crouched in the container, was the enormous hairy spider. A gasp went up from the audience. Charlotte's camera flashed again and the audience began clapping with great enthusiasm. Few of the people there had ever dared hope they would see a living Devil Spider.

Click.

The lights went out. It was suddenly pitch black in the hall. For a moment, the audience sat in stunned silence. Then a harsh voice shouted:

"If you know what's good for you, NOBODY MOVE!"

Of course nobody obeyed. There was the sound of people twisting and turning in their chairs, trying to see who had shouted this extraordinary order; and a buzz of nervous chatter. Was this a joke?

"I warned you!" the shrill, disembodied voice shrieked.

HissssssssssssssSSSSsssssssssssssSSSSSSSsssssss.

The slow hissing sound was followed by a muffled thump.

"It's a smoke bomb!" someone yelled. Suddenly, panic struck the entire audience as they found they couldn't breathe. They coughed and spluttered and fought their way towards the exit.

The dark shadows of three figures pushed their way against the general rush and climbed up onto the stage. Every few seconds, Charlotte's camera flash lit the scene. Caught in the glare of this were two ugly thugs in black leather coats running towards Thaddeus.

"What do you want?" demanded Thaddeus, desperately trying to refocus his eyes after the flash of light.

The men wasted no time with talking. In the next flash of light Charlotte could see Thaddeus lashing out as they wrestled him to the floor. Screams of fear, shouts of anger, and wracking coughs came from the panic-stricken audience. Charlotte's camera flashes made the struggle on stage appear almost unreal.

Then, suddenly, the lights came on again. To everyone's astonishment the intruders were nowhere to be seen.

Charlotte, her cameras hanging round her neck, saw Thaddeus lying beside the table and clambered up to him. A trickle of blood ran from his nose as he slowly got to his feet.

"Thaddeus! Are you all right?" she asked, worried. She fished in her pocket for a handkerchief, and put an arm round his waist. But he wasn't listening. He was staring at something.

Charlotte followed his horrified gaze. The spider and its case were gone!

"Operation Devil successfully accomplished, Master. But—" Block pressed the mobile phone to his ear as the van screeched round a corner at high speed. He gripped the transparent box containing the Devil Spider between his knees as he was flung heavily against the door. He glared at the driver. His mouth twitched and his head jerked violently. "But that journalist woman was there taking photographs," he managed to blurt out.

There was a moment of relative calm at the other end of the line as Clovis Monk thought aloud. "Charlotte Clancy, eh? So, our paths cross once more. BRING HER TO ME, Block."

Block flinched as his boss screamed instructions down the phone.

"Yes, Mr Monk," he whined. "Capture her... Bring her to Killimooin... Yes, Master... No foul-ups..." He clicked off the phone and shoved it into his pocket.

As always, Block – the thug who had stolen the spider – was dressed entirely in black. He wore a leather coat, a trilby hat pulled so low on his forehead that it touched the top of his black-rimmed glasses, a polo-neck jumper, black trousers, highly polished shoes, and leather gloves. He gulped and dabbed nervously at the sweat dripping from beneath the brim of his hat. He turned to the driver. "Go back, Toad!" he ordered in his high-pitched, nasal voice. "We have to get the woman!"

CHAPTER TWO

"Just how dangerous is the Devil Spider?" asked Charlotte as she held her front door open for Thaddeus.

"Deadly," he said, dropping his overnight bag in the hall and following her through to the living room. "In a small animal, it causes instant paralysis. But the Maluku Devil is unique. It carries an antidote to its own poison in a separate sac under its throat. So, if it wants to, it can prevent its victim from dying."

Charlotte frowned. "Why on earth would it want to do that?"

"Oh, to keep its food fresh and tangy until it's hungry." Thaddeus smiled wryly. "It catches frogs and mice and keeps them alive in holes underground."

Charlotte screwed up her face in disgust. "What does it do to humans?"

"Well, we're bigger and stronger than its usual prey. First of all we would suffer periodic blackouts. Then creeping paralysis. And if the antidote is not given within forty-eight hours" – Thaddeus snapped his fingers with a loud crack – "you've had it."

Charlotte shuddered. "Ugh! Gruesome. Who

do you think would want to steal such a vile creature?" she asked.

Thaddeus shrugged his shoulders. "A drug company, military research, maybe... a collector of rare species... Who knows?"

Charlotte slung her jacket onto the armchair and gestured Thaddeus towards the door at the end of the room. "I had my films sent over to my assistant while the nurse was patching up your nose. She promised to develop the photos before she left for lunch."

They went into the eerie red glow of her darkroom. After checking there were no prints left in the developing fluid, she switched on the main light.

A stack of new prints lay on the workbench and others were pegged up to dry on a wire above them.

"Now," said Charlotte, tugging down one of the prints, "let's see what we have here."

Thaddeus began to sift through the pile at her side.

"Hey!" said Charlotte, tapping the photograph. "I know this guy!"

"Ms Clancy!" said Thaddeus, pretending to be shocked. "I had no idea your circle of friends included great big hairy spider-nappers!"

"Oh, shut up!" she laughed. "His name is

Damien Block. Always wears black. He's a loathsome, weasely piece of work, and he's got an awful twitch which gets worse when he's nervous. It'd be tragic if he wasn't such a revolting creature. Actually, now I come to think of it, I realise it was his voice in the hall earlier. It has a high-pitched nasal sound... He used to work for a weirdo medical scientist called Clovis Monk."

Thaddeus frowned. "Clovis Monk... that sounds familiar."

"Yep. A few years back he was involved in a big court case. He was accused of attempting to poison his partner with—"

Thaddeus's eyes widened as he remembered the case. "Snake venom!"

"Yes, but it could never be proved and he wasn't convicted," Charlotte said, shaking her head in disgust.

Thaddeus looked at her curiously. "You're very well informed, Charlotte. How—?"

"Ah, well, he was only brought to trial because his activities were exposed in a newspaper. And the investigative journalist on his case was" – Charlotte smiled and pointed at herself – "yours truly."

Thaddeus looked suitably impressed and, leaning back against the counter, asked, "So where's Clovis Monk now?"

"No one knows," she said, glancing at her watch. "He left the country and hasn't been heard of since. Thaddeus, you realise it's one o'clock?"

He looked at her blankly, surprised by the sudden change of topic.

"Your kids. Airport. Baronia," Charlotte prompted.

"Oh, no!" he gasped, slapping the palm of his hand against his forehead. "You're an angel, Charlotte. They'll never forgive me if they miss their flight," he said, dashing out of the room.

"Yes, yes, I know... Give my love to the little monsters," she called after him.

"Do you think Dad's forgotten?" Mike asked his elder sister anxiously.

"No, of course not!" Peggy reassured him, though secretly she half suspected he had.

Mike drummed his fingers on the table. "Why is he late then?"

Ruby ruffled his hair. "Don't worry, honey, he and Charlotte were probably held up at the conference."

Mike looked up at her. "Do you think he likes Charlotte?"

"I like her," said Laura, "I wish she and Dad

were coming with us."

"Yes, except they do argue quite a bit," put in Jack.

Peggy rolled her eyes. "Oh, Jack, all grown-ups argue— Hey! I think I can hear…"

Mike leapt up and bounded towards the door. "It's Dad!" he yelled, and they all raced out to meet the car.

Mike, Laura and Peggy rushed to hug their father as he stepped down from the Land Rover. Ruby and Jack hung back, grinning at the excited bundle of Arnolds. Although Jack was no relation, he lived with the Arnold family because he had no father or mother. The children treated him like a brother, but he always let them greet their father first.

"Where've you been, Dad?" asked Peggy, giving his hand a good squeeze.

Laura pulled at his other arm. "Yes, Dad, what if the plane leaves without us?"

Thaddeus laughed. "They wouldn't dare! Besides, I bet you lot aren't even packed yet, are you?" He winked at Ruby.

"We've been packed for ages," cried Mike.

"What? Everything? Toothbrushes? Towels? Socks?" Thaddeus feigned disbelief.

"Y-e-s!" they all chorused.

"Elephant traps?" Thaddeus continued as the

children's eyes widened. "Tiger repellent?"

They clicked. "Oh, Dad!" they all said at once and ran off, laughing, to get their bags.

CHAPTER THREE

"So, Block, what are you up to this time, stealing a poisonous spider?" Charlotte was thinking aloud when she heard something move in the next room. She kept very still and listened carefully.

"Thaddeus?" she called after a moment. "Did you forget something?" She opened the darkroom door and peered out. "Thaddeus?"

Charlotte froze. It wasn't Thaddeus! She was face to face with the ghastly, twitching Damien Block! His eyes narrowed and he put on a false smile. His head jerked crookedly to one side and his lip curled in a nasty sneer.

"Good afternoon, Ms Clancy," he whined, faking politeness.

Before Charlotte could utter a word or step back she heard a hiss and felt the sting of cold spray on her face.

For a moment, she stood in a daze, then slumped into a woozy heap on the floor. The photographs she had been examining dropped from her hand and spilled like a pack of cards across the floor.

Block chuckled with satisfaction. "Thank you, Ms Clancy. Most helpful of you," he said, raising his hat sarcastically and snorting with laughter at his own joke.

He put down the briefcase he was carrying, stepped over Charlotte and hurried into the darkroom. Sweeping the incriminating photographs of himself into a pile, he flung everything else impatiently onto the floor.

Charlotte felt her body was heavy enough to sink through the floorboards; her brain was hot and fuzzy. She could hear Block moving about in the darkroom but it was as if he were miles away. Drifting in and out of consciousness, she could sense Block kneeling nearby. With an almighty effort she managed to half open her eyes. She could just make out his blurry figure as he gathered up the scattered photographs.

With another supreme effort of will she levered herself up onto one elbow. But it was no good. A terrible dizziness overcame her and she collapsed, knocking Block's briefcase to the floor as she fell. It toppled over, spilling its contents across the carpet. Block, cursing wildly, gathered the papers up in a state of nervous frenzy.

At last, everything was stuffed into the briefcase. Block pulled out his mobile phone, and hissed into it.

"Toad, bring the van round the back. We have to get her out without being seen. We'll crate her up at the warehouse, and freight her out to Baronia from there."

Block looked at Charlotte's slumped body for a moment, then slung her roughly over his shoulder and left as quietly as possible.

He did not notice that a shipping document had fluttered from his briefcase and slipped under the sofa.

The small passenger plane made a perfect landing and halted smoothly on the runway. Ruby, the children, and Prince, all looking rather dishevelled after their three-hour flight, tumbled down the gangway onto the tarmac.

"Baronia, here we come!" whooped Mike.

A black limousine drew up in front of them and a tall, gangly boy with curly brown hair leapt out to greet them.

"Hello, everyone... Wow! I can hardly believe you're really here!" he said. His hand shot up suddenly as something wet and rough touched it. He knelt and threw his arms joyfully round the Arnold's dog. "Prince! Hello, boy!"

A hefty, middle-aged man dressed in a plaid shirt, jeans and cowboy boots stepped out of the car. Prince Paul rolled his eyes and nodded in the stranger's direction. "Oh, yes," he said ruefully, "this is Barney Stokes, my bodyguard. Ex-US

Secret Service."

The man stepped forward, his eyes twinkling beneath bushy eyebrows. "Hi, folks. Ma'am – you must be Ruby? Pleasure to meet you all."

Their luggage was soon loaded into the limousine's spacious boot, and Ruby and the children into its luxurious interior.

"Cor!" sighed Jack, gulping down a freshly-squeezed mango and lime juice from the well-stocked fridge. "I wouldn't mind being a prince if I could have a car like this!"

They sped through the beautiful Baronian countryside, and were soon at the gates of the magnificent royal Palace.

Two guards, dressed in red livery, opened the double doors to the State Chamber and ushered in the children, Prince and, last of all, Ruby. At the far end of the room, on an ornate golden throne, sat the King of Baronia. He looked dauntingly impressive, dressed in a dark uniform with a magisterial sash and a row of medals across his chest.

Prince Paul prodded Ruby forward, and whispered, "Did Jack tell you how to address my father?"

Ruby gulped and nodded her head nervously. After a few hesitant steps, she strode boldly down the long red carpet.

"Your Majesty!" she cried, kneeling respectfully at his feet. She quickly slipped a shoe off his foot and threw it over her shoulder. "The King's feet go everywhere!" she proclaimed.

The King stared at her in stunned silence. Ruby feared she had made a terrible *faux pas*. Slowly, a look of understanding began to creep across his face.

The King wriggled his toes in amusement. "I think, my dear," he said, patting her shoulder reassuringly, "you've been the victim of one of Paul's little jokes!"

The children could no longer contain themselves. Their stifled giggles burst out in uncontrollable laughter and, to their great relief, the King was good-naturedly joining in.

"You little beasts!" said Ruby, turning towards them with her hands on her hips. But she was so relieved that she had not offended the King that she couldn't help laughing herself.

A few miles away, a guard was thrust into a cavernous underground laboratory. The young man, horrified by what he had seen going on deep beneath the Secret Forest of Killimooin, had been caught trying to escape.

"You snivelling little deserter!" roared his commander, dressed, like all the guards, in camouflage gear with a balaclava masking most of his face. He shoved the prisoner into a chair. "Sit there and keep your mouth shut!"

The electronically-controlled door slid open abruptly. The commander stood stiffly to attention and gave a sharp, military salute. In rapid-fire delivery he announced, "Fugitive apprehended in Killimooin Mountains, sir."

The bearded man who'd entered the lab was tall, about fifty, with straight, grey hair that fell halfway down his back. His eyes were such a bright blue that his pockmarked skin was hardly noticeable. Immaculately dressed in a loose white linen suit and white brogues, this was Clovis Monk, the mastermind behind the spider robbery.

He smiled crazily at the prisoner as he reached for his swivel chair. He sat down and swung round to his desk. Glass test tubes, bottles, Petri dishes, various implements and medical paraphernalia were neatly laid out along it.

Monk pulled a small glass case towards him, held it up to the light and for a moment stared at the spider inside. He swung round and snarled at the captured young guard, "Such a pity – for you!" He turned to the other guards and barked, "Hold him down!"

"Now, my precious," said Monk, suddenly

tender. "It would only be polite to introduce yourself to our deserter." He moved towards the captive and flicked up the lid of the case. The blood drained from the young man's face and he began to squirm, and then to scream in terror.

"Let it be known among all the guards," boomed Monk, "that there is only one penalty for desertion!" He released the Maluku Devil Spider onto the man's arm and smiled cruelly as it plunged its pincers into the warm, trembling flesh.

Monk threw back his head, laughing triumphantly, his eyes glittering with madness.

CHAPTER FOUR

Some time later, Clovis Monk was studying one of the many video screens above his desk. Each one showed a different area of the Secret Forest, relayed by surveillance cameras that were constantly scanning every section. The two uniformed guards on either side of his table didn't move as Block burst into the room.

Twitching and trembling, he fell to his knees in front of Monk. "Master, I am returned," he snivelled.

Monk looked down with disgust at the man grovelling at his feet. "The merchandise. Give it to me!" he commanded, thrusting out his hand.

Block drew out the box and, with infinite care, placed it in Monk's hands.

"Ahh, ahh… exquisite!" Monk almost purred with pleasure as he stroked the box. "Now we have a mate for my other Devil Spider. Soon we shall no longer have to hide like fugitives under the Secret Forest of Killimooin."

Monk wrenched his gaze away from the spider and turned back to Block. In a friendly tone, he asked, "And the Clancy woman?"

Block's mouth twitched nervously, showing his yellow teeth. "She's arriving with our regular freight delivery tomorrow night, Master."

"Good... Good, Block... Now..." Monk turned his glittering eyes once more to the spider, and spoke quietly. "The Queen of the Maluku Devils. But will she give us the antidote?" He placed the transparent container gently on the table, selected a syringe and inserted the needle into the spider's sac.

As a pale green liquid was drawn up into the tube of the syringe, Monk's eyes blazed with excitement. When the tube was full, he slowly withdrew the needle. He transferred the antidote to a test tube and turned to the slumped body of the captured guard. "Now," he said, "the question is: will her antidote counteract the poison of another spider?"

Monk lifted the young man's limp head and trickled the pale liquid into his mouth. "If I'm right," said Monk, "he should recover within seconds."

The guard spluttered and moaned.

"Aha! I knew it!" Monk cried triumphantly. "Take him away and watch him carefully," he ordered. He sank back against the chair and closed his eyes to savour the moment.

Block, unsure whether this meant he was dismissed, dithered about uneasily in front of his master. He shivered violently when Monk's eyes snapped open and bored into him. "I-I-I—" he stuttered.

Monk held up his hand. "We're doing well, Block."

Block exhaled and giggled nervously in agreement.

"Exceptionally well."

Block felt all the tension draining away. "M-master, I've been informed there will be visitors to the royal Killimooin Lodge tomorrow."

"I know," said Monk, thoughtfully. "Most unwelcome. But they won't be staying long!" He smiled. "I've prepared a little welcome committee for them. A hairy one!" he added, gloating to himself.

Block stared at him for a moment and then, with a nervous spasm of head jerks and facial twitches, he rubbed his hands together and cackled like a hyena.

Barney led the party on the long trek through the forest from the Palace to Killimooin Lodge. They'd been walking for at least two hours and were still chattering excitedly after the nerve-tingling experience of crossing a swaying rope bridge suspended high up over a steep ravine with a river rushing way, way below them.

Jack shifted his backpack, and huffed, "How

much further to go, Barney?"

"About half an hour," Barney called heartily over his shoulder. "How are you doing back there, Ruby?" he added, turning to wait for her to catch up.

"Let's just say," puffed Ruby, "that these legs were made for dancing, not hiking."

"Sounds like you could do with a break, little lady. Whoa there, everyone. Take a breather." He handed Ruby a flask of water and she gulped it down thirstily.

The five children stood a short distance away in the shade of a tall tree. Mike was eyeing Barney. "I still don't see why we need him," he said.

"It's only Dad fussing," explained Paul, kicking a tuft of grass.

"But what's he supposed to be protecting us from?" Jack asked Paul, as Barney and Ruby started walking towards them.

"The King said I wasn't to take my eyes off you lot," Barney told them with a grin on his face.

Paul looked astonished. "You mean we won't be able to go off exploring on our own at all?"

Barney shook his head. "Sorry, Prince Paul, but orders are orders."

*

A hand reached up to lever open one of the windows of Killimooin Lodge. A man hoisted himself nimbly up onto the ledge and jumped soundlessly into the room. He tiptoed stealthily to the main bedroom where he flipped a small knapsack from his back. Very slowly, he took out a transparent box. The light caught its edges, making it glint like an enormous jewel. He opened the lid cautiously and tipped the hideous creature it contained gently onto the duvet. The spider, sensing freedom, immediately scuttled to the furthest end of the bed and hid itself beneath the duvet.

The sound of voices outside the lodge stirred the man to action. He turned and left the lodge as quickly and silently as he had entered.

When he was safely back in the forest, virtually invisible in his camouflage gear and balaclava, he spoke quietly into his mobile phone. "Welcome committee operational. I'm coming out."

Her front door was ajar!

"Charlotte?" Thaddeus called, suddenly extremely anxious. He had left several messages on her answerphone the previous evening, and when she still had not phoned him the next morning, he had decided to call round. He pushed the door open with his fingertips and let it squeak back on its hinges. He stepped forward cautiously, calling her name again, with more urgency this time. The flat was deathly quiet.

"What on earth…?"

Thaddeus hurried past the upturned chair and into the ransacked darkroom. He stared in disbelief at the chaos of photographic equipment and papers littered everywhere. He bent down quickly to scrabble through the mess on the floor. There was not a single negative or photograph left of yesterday's spider robbery!

He slumped down on a sofa in the adjoining room, his brain racing. He rested his chin on his hands, trying to work out what might have happened. A piece of paper fluttered on the floor beside him. He flicked it out from under the sofa with the heel of his shoe. It was a shipping invoice – and it certainly wasn't Charlotte's. The logo at the top read UNIVERSAL STORAGE & SHIPPING COMPANY.

Twenty minutes later Thaddeus was creeping past two burly thugs who were chatting over steaming mugs of tea in the company's guard box. He ducked below their window and sneaked into the warehouse, taking cover for a moment behind a wooden shipping crate. He had no idea what to expect or even what to look for. But if, as he suspected, Charlotte had been kidnapped by the same people who had taken the spider and the incriminating photographs, this seemed to be the only possible place to begin his search for her.

The warehouse was the size of an aircraft hanger. Row upon row of wooden crates and cardboard boxes were stacked floor to ceiling. Thaddeus wondered how this place and Charlotte's disappearance were connected.

C-R-A-C-K!

Someone was coming! Thaddeus crept backwards down one of the aisles, away from the noise. His fingers ran along the stacked boxes to guide him steadily round the corner at the end. All the while, his eyes were fixed ahead on the aisle in front of him.

"Oof!" He collided into someone who was backing round the stack from the opposite direction. He turned round instantly, ready to do battle.

CHAPTER FIVE

"Charlotte!"

"Thaddeus!"

They beamed at one another. "Oh, you gave me a shock!" she whispered. "I thought you were one of Block's ghastly henchmen! They locked me in a wooden crate. I've only just managed to cut my way out – using a two-inch nail!"

"Shhh!" Thaddeus whispered fiercely, pulling her towards him. "Someone's coming!"

"There she is! You go that way. Cut her off!" shouted one of the thugs.

Charlotte and Thaddeus raced off, skidding round the corners of each aisle as they ran along in search of an exit. From the angry shouts of their pursuers, it was evident that they had only seen Charlotte.

As Thaddeus slid round a corner in front of her, Charlotte gripped the edge of a low box and ripped it from its stack. An avalanche of boxes followed and effectively blocked the aisle behind them.

Thaddeus turned to Charlotte and panted out, "Well done, that ought to give us time to—"

Without warning, Charlotte seemed to judder

and blur in front of his eyes. He felt sick to the stomach and reached out a weak arm in an attempt to support himself. A thick mist seemed to be enveloping him. The last hazy thing he saw as he fainted to the floor was the look of alarm on Charlotte's face as she came towards him in what seemed unbearably slow motion.

"Oh! Thaddeus! Thaddeus! What's the matter?" hissed Charlotte, kneeling beside him. She tried desperately to shake him back into consciousness but she could not revive him. She had to act fast. Gripping his shoulders, she dragged him behind a stack of boxes, shoved an extra couple in front to conceal his feet, and ran straight into the clutches of the two men who grabbed her as she swung into one of the aisles. She struggled hard, and managed to knock one of the men down, but she was no match for two of them. Neither of the men noticed that a wallet had fallen to the floor from one of their jacket pockets.

Behind the stack of boxes, Thaddeus began to drift back into consciousness and listened helplessly to the scuffle as the two men bundled Charlotte away.

For the second time in two days, Charlotte found herself being dumped in a shipping crate.

"Let me out of here, you morons!" she yelled, pummelling the side of the crate. She pressed her ear to the rough wooden slats, and could just make out the tail-end of the guards' conversation.

"Block says we've got to get her to Baronia sharpish. Load her up with the other crates for delivery tonight."

"Baronia!" thought Charlotte, but had no time to consider what this meant before she heard the splutter and chug of a fork-lift truck starting up. She braced herself, which was just as well, because the next second the crate she was in swayed violently forward and then crashed back. There was a sharp bump and Charlotte felt the whole thing slowly ascend. Then came the sensation of moving forward and turning a corner before being dropped.

Another engine rumbled into life underneath her and the crate juddered. "I must be in the delivery lorry!" thought Charlotte. She began to sweep her hands across the walls of her small prison in search of something – anything – that might aid her escape.

As the lorry rolled forward towards the exit a dishevelled figure staggered up behind it and, making a superhuman effort, hauled himself over the tailboard.

"Charlotte? Can you hear me, Charlotte?"

Thaddeus's voice sounded as if he were right next to her.

"Thaddeus!" Charlotte said in amazement. "How did you get in here? What happened? Are you all right?"

He leant closer to the crate and whispered, "I don't know, I just sort of blacked out— Oh no!" An awful thought occurred to him and he pulled up his sleeves.

"What?" hissed Charlotte, sounding alarmed.

Thaddeus stared in silent horror at the two very visible puncture wounds on his left wrist.

"Thaddeus? Are you there?" Charlotte was frightened now.

"Yes," Thaddeus said hoarsely, "I'm here. But I don't know for how long."

"What do you mean?" said Charlotte. She could hardly breathe.

"I made a grab for the spider when I was wrestling with Block. It's bitten me."

Charlotte's heart skipped a beat.

"Thaddeus," she said, almost too scared to hear the answer. "What exactly does that mean?"

Thaddeus slumped wearily to the floor. He reached into his pocket and took out the guard's wallet. He'd picked it up in the warehouse after he'd come round from his blackout. In it he found a card with a black security strip on one side. He flipped it over and examined it curiously in the poor light. Emblazoned with a bright red spider emblem, it bore in shimmering silver letters the words "Clovis Monk Laboratories".

"It means," Thaddeus said after a moment's thought, "we're in big trouble."

With a grand sweep of his arm, Barney announced, "Ladies and gentlemen, I give you... the royal Killimooin Lodge."

The children and Ruby had just emerged panting from a long uphill climb through dense undergrowth and now found themselves on a gently undulating lawn, peppered with clumps of exotic flowering shrubs. A beautiful wooden building with a long elegant veranda nestled among them.

"Wow!" – "Cor!" – "Fantastic!" They all gasped in admiration.

"Come on," said Paul proudly. "I'll show you round."

The children dumped their backpacks and, with Prince yelping excitedly round their heels, they set off to explore.

"Don't go beyond the fences, OK?" Barney instructed. He picked up their bags and turned to Ruby. "Follow me, ma'am. You sure do look beat!"

Ten minutes later Ruby took great delight in flopping down in an exhausted heap. Kicking off her shoes, she sank happily into the luxury of the bed's plumped-up feather duvet and dreamily soft pillow. This was more like it! She closed her eyes and sighed with pleasure.

The boys left Peggy and Laura feeding the swans on the river while they wandered up to the barn.

"Wow!" said Jack, running over to an ancient motorbike. "What a humdinger!"

"Dad rode it when he was young. And it's kept tuned up now, ready for me when I'm old enough," said Paul, holding it steady while Jack clambered on.

Mike picked up some old motorcycle goggles. "Brilliant. Can I—"

"Aaaaagh-aaaagh! Aaaaaagh-aaaaagh!"

A bone-chilling, bloodcurdling scream suddenly rent the air.

"Blimey!" gulped Mike, his eyes popping. "What was that?"

For a moment, they stared at one another. Then, all at once, they knew. "RUBY!" they shouted together.

CHAPTER SIX

White-faced and trembling, Ruby was cowering in the far corner of her room, pointing at the bed. "It m-m-must have been under the duvet," she stuttered, shuddering at the thought.

Jack put a comforting arm round her. "It's OK, Rube, it's only a spider."

"But l-l-look at the size of it!" she gasped.

With his free hand Jack gave his younger friend a gentle shove. "Mike, pass me that glass."

He positioned it carefully over the spider, slipped a magazine under it, and picked the whole thing up to examine it.

"What a beauty!" he admired as the others clustered round.

"Gee, ma'am, that was some scary scream. You all right?" said Barney, appearing in the doorway.

Ruby's only reply was to point a quivering finger.

As Mike held up the glass for Barney's inspection, Paul, looking puzzled, said, "I don't understand it. We don't have spiders like that in Baronia."

"Well, you do now," said Barney. "And I've seen critters like that in the Far East. You don't mess with them, folks, they're deadly. We've got to leave." He looked seriously worried.

"Leave!" snapped Paul. "Because of a spider! That's ridiculous!"

"The whole place could be infested," Barney warned.

Paul threw up his hands in disbelief.

Ruby, having recovered somewhat, suggested a compromise. "Why don't we give the lodge a thorough search? If we find any more spiders, we'll go. If we don't, we'll stay."

She looked quizzically at Barney as he considered the proposal. "Come on, Barn," Ruby cajoled, nudging his arm, "If I can live with a few spiders, then surely an experienced secret serviceman like you can handle it!"

He smiled bashfully. "Well, OK... On condition you don't go back on your word!"

"Oomph!" Peggy dumped an armful of firewood into the wicker basket. "Where's Laura?" she asked, straightening up.

"Don't know," said Mike, dropping his load onto the pile and wiping his hands on his trousers. "Do you, Paul?"

"After Barney gave the all-clear to stay, I saw her hot-footing it into the forest after Prince. I think she was trying to rescue a rabbit from him," said Paul.

Jack grinned. "A perfect excuse for avoiding work, if you ask me! I volunteer her for all the clearing up when she gets back!" The four of them laughed in agreement and wandered outside to look for her.

Damien Block, underground in the Secret Forest, stepped through an electronic door and stood twitching nervously in Monk's laboratory. "You sent for me, Master," he whined.

"Yes, Block. It is essential we have no distractions for the next few days. Take a couple of guards up to Killimooin Lodge and make sure our visitors have gone."

Block jerked alarmingly as he said, "At once, Master," and turned to make his way up through the maze of underground passages to ground level.

"WOW!" gasped Laura. Hot on Prince's trail, she had plunged headlong through a dense pocket of undergrowth and found herself crouching in the low entrance to a cave. She hesitated for a moment, twisting one of her ribbons thoughtfully round her finger. She knew she should go and get the others to explore it with her, but curiosity got the better of her. She stepped inside, blinking until her eyes adjusted to the gloom, and skimming one of her hands along the rough-hewn walls to guide her.

Suddenly, she came to an abrupt halt, and her mouth dropped open in amazement.

"B-L-I-M-E-Y!" she exclaimed in a breathless whisper.

Bathed in an eerie light at the end of the cave, towering over her, was an enormous, ancient-looking stone statue. A long pair of carved wings were folded across its body from head to toe.

As Laura took a step forward to investigate she was almost knocked off her feet. Prince hurtled into her, barking like mad.

"What's the matter with you?" she said sternly, turning round and trying to grab his collar. "Where have you been, you naughty dog?"

Prince dipped his head and danced about her, growling and barking in a frenzy.

Laura stamped her foot impatiently. "Prince! Don't growl at me, you wretched animal! Come here! Bad dog!"

But he barked again, even more loudly than before. The statue behind Laura had opened up, and Prince could see a long tunnel winding away into the distance. The statue was a secret door!

Laura hadn't seen it yet. "Prince, you stupid

beast, come here, or I'll—"

"Seize her!" A high-pitched, nasally voice screamed from behind her.

Laura felt herself being hoisted from the ground and dragged backwards towards the statue. "Hey! Let me go!" she shouted, twisting her head from side to side and struggling for all she was worth.

Two men wearing camouflage uniforms gripped her arms tightly and did their best to avoid her flailing feet. Another man, dressed all in black, his bespectacled face twitching angrily, stood in the cavern shouting instructions at the guards.

"Prince!" screamed Laura desperately. "Fetch! Fetch Jack! Fetch Peggy! GO!"

As Prince took to his heels, she was dragged, kicking and screaming, through the entrance into a neon-lit tunnel. The wings of the statue closed and the cavern was silent once more.

Back at the lodge, Jack and Paul met up with Ruby and Barney.

"Any luck?" asked Ruby anxiously.

Paul shook his head, just as worried as she was. "Not a sign of her anywhere." He turned to the others who all shook their heads.

"Peggy and I searched the buildings at the

back of the lodge. Nothing," said Mike.

Peggy frowned. "What now, then?" she asked.

All eyes turned to Barney. He hesitated for a moment, and then said, "I reckon we ought to search this part of the mountain. If Laura's lost her way or had a fall, I'd bet my bottom dollar it'd be here. I say we—"

"Prince!" yelped Peggy. The collie came bounding out of the undergrowth and began whining, and pawing feverishly at their ankles.

Jack bent down and stroked his head reassuringly. "Do you know where Laura is, Prince? Where's Laura? LAURA?" he urged hopefully.

Prince barked sharply at the sound of her name, and backed away towards the forest track from which he had just emerged.

"He does!" cried Peggy. "I'm sure he wants us to follow him, look!"

"Well," said Barney, "he's going our way. Why not?"

Before he'd even finished the sentence the children had raced off after their dog. Barney and Ruby followed at a brisk pace.

CHAPTER SEVEN

After half an hour of tramping through the mountainous woodland, Barney halted the search party. The three boys were still some distance ahead, scrambling after Prince. "I think we've come far enough, folks," said Barney. He cupped his hands to his mouth and shouted for the boys to return.

"Dad will be furious, if we've allowed Laura to get lost. And, besides, Prince obviously still wants us to follow him!" cried Peggy.

"That's for sure," said Barney. "But I think he just wants to take us for a walk!"

Paul, who'd reached them just in time to hear the last two remarks, stamped his foot with royal impatience. "He does NOT! He's taking us to Laura!"

"Well, maybe," said Barney doubtfully. "But from here on, the mountain gets dangerous. We have to turn back," he insisted.

"Well, you do what you like. I'm going on!" Paul hissed angrily and stomped off.

"Paul!" Ruby called after him, but he ignored her.

Barney, in a conciliatory tone pleaded, "Paul, please! This isn't helping any."

Paul continued to walk away and Barney finally resorted to threats: "If you don't come back right now, young man, I will have to tell your father!"

Paul, enraged, stopped and turned to face him. "GOOD!" he said defiantly. "And you can tell him that you couldn't even be bothered to look for my friend!" He turned round and stormed off down the forest track.

"PAUL! Come back here, you—"

Barney was interrupted by the sudden appearance of Jack who had burst out of the bushes, spluttering with excitement. "Quick! Down here!" he yelled, pointing to the cave that Laura had found. The others rushed after him, into the darkness.

Ruby took one look at the statue and gave a long whistle. Prince barked and scratched like a mad thing at its base.

"What is it?" said Peggy, trying to silence the frantic dog.

Paul stepped forward to examine the statue. "This is Voltan, King of the Underworld. Ancient Baronians feared him more than any of the seven Gods of Wrath." He looked over his shoulder at them. "People say if you touch statues like this, you die."

Jack gulped nervously and took a step back.

"You don't believe that, do you?" he said, trying to hide his fear.

"No, of course not!" Paul dismissed the old myth.

Barney interrupted. "Come on, folks. This statue is not going to help us find Laura."

"Hey, look! It's Laura's hair ribbon!" cried Peggy, bending down to pick it up.

"You see!" said Paul, "Prince *is* trying to lead us to her!"

"Oh, come on, Paul," said Barney in disbelief. He grabbed Prince's collar. "He could have brought that in here himself. I'm sorry, but enough is enough. We've got to go back to the lodge." He began to herd the reluctant party out of the cave. "I'll phone the Royal Guard," he assured Paul, "and have them come and do a search, OK?"

The lorry jolted up and down and swayed from side to side as it wound its way through the Baronian mountains. Thaddeus was finding it difficult to stay upright as he struggled to prise open the lid of Charlotte's crate.

"Ugh," he groaned, staggered slightly, and suddenly fainted.

"Thaddeus?" whispered Charlotte urgently. "Are you all right?"

Thaddeus slid to the floor, trying to banish the all-engulfing dizziness. Slowly, he pulled himself upright again and, in as bright a voice as he could muster, said, "It's no good, the blasted thing is well and truly nailed down."

"Never mind that," hissed Charlotte. "You have to get yourself to a hospital."

Thaddeus leant heavily against the crate, but this time could not keep the weariness from his voice. "No point. The only thing that will work is the spider's antidote."

Inside the crate, Charlotte was quiet for a moment, and then asked, "So, what are we going to do?"

Thaddeus drummed his fingers on the crate. "Well, we don't have much option. We have to stay in this lorry. These men are acting on Block's orders and, presumably, he is acting on Monk's. With any luck they'll take us to the spider."

For a long while they were both silent. Thaddeus lay on a stack of tarpaulins and closed his eyes. The rumble and momentum of the lorry was making him sleepy. Before too long he lapsed once more into unconsciousness.

Half an hour later Charlotte was whispering urgently, "Thaddeus? Thaddeus? THADDEUS!"

Pressing his knuckles into bleary eyes,

Thaddeus answered foggily, "Ye-e-s?"

Charlotte sighed with relief when she heard his voice. "You must have blacked out again, Thad."

"What?... Yes." Slowly, Thaddeus began to remember where he was. "Yes, I must have."

"We stopped quite a while ago. I don't think we're there yet, but luckily no one's come," Charlotte whispered.

Thaddeus realised with horror that she was right. "I'll check it out," he said, and peered cautiously over the tailgate of the lorry.

The two men were some distance away, sitting at a picnic table and reading comics as they slurped from a thermos flask and munched sandwiches. Thaddeus slipped down from the lorry and crept along the side furthest from them. He stood on tiptoe to peer into the cab. A mobile phone lay tantalisingly on the seat. He inched open the door and slid his hand towards it. Just as his fingers closed round the base, it trilled startlingly loudly.

Slithering down in alarm, Thaddeus saw one of the thugs leap up from his bench and hurry towards the lorry. Thaddeus clicked the door shut and flattened himself against it, hardly daring to breathe. He strained to hear what was being said, but the windows were wound up and all he heard was the man eventually call his companion to get back into the lorry.

Thaddeus inched his way to the back of the lorry. But too late! The other thug's shadow fell across the ground as he came towards the end of the vehicle.

Thaddeus froze. Any second now the man would turn the corner and discover him! There was only one place to hide. He dived under the lorry and lay without moving against one of the enormous tyres. The thug's feet passed by without pausing, and disappeared as he hitched himself up into the cab. Thaddeus breathed a sigh of relief, but the next moment he was rigid with horror. The engine had roared into life and the lorry began to move forward, slowly gathering speed – with Thaddeus underneath!

CHAPTER EIGHT

Thaddeus ducked his head and rolled at high speed to the centre of the axle. He flipped his body slightly to one side and scooted his body along with his feet as the lorry turned and, thank goodness, left him with nothing but beautiful blue sky above him. He picked himself up and sprinted after the lorry as it moved onto the main road. Gathering all his strength, he launched himself at the tailgate. He grabbed at it and dragged his feet up onto the tow-hook for support. He swung up and fell with a thud into the back.

"Thaddeus? Is that you? What happened? Are you all right?" whispered Charlotte.

Thaddeus leant against the crate, regaining his breath. He put his hands in his pockets to warm them and heard the jangle of coins. He pulled one out and looked at it thoughtfully.

"Charlotte?"

"Yes?"

"I think I may be able to get you out after all."

The guards had taken Laura far into Monk's underground headquarters, to a spotlessly clean and empty laboratory.

"Who are you? What do you want with me?" cried Laura angrily to Block. "You wait till my father hears about this!"

"Sit there, you nasty little girl," snapped Block, twitching agitatedly. "And shut up! Your natter, natter, natter is getting on my nerves!"

The two guards forced Laura into a chair. She pushed up the glasses that had been teetering on the end of her nose as the men dragged her along the endless underground corridors. Gazing silently round, she shuddered at the sight of an enormous spider in a glass box. It was very similar to the one they'd captured in Ruby's room.

And come to think of it, she mused, it's just like the Maluku Devil that Dad brought back from—

Her thoughts were interrupted by the arrival of a tall man in a white suit. His eyes bored into her.

"So, what have we here?" he asked dryly.

Block stooped forward slightly, as though bowing respectfully to a king, and cleared his throat uneasily. "She was in the cave, Master. I thought it wise to come straight back."

Monk glared at Laura. "Who are you? What are you doing here?"

Laura crossed her arms and stared back at him defiantly.

Infuriated that she seemed totally uncowed, his tone hardened and he shouted savagely, "You have a tongue. USE IT!"

"My name is Laura Arnold. I'm from England, and you have no right to keep me prisoner!"

She stood up to leave, but Block pressed her firmly back onto the chair.

"Young lady, you are in no position to lecture me!" sneered Monk. "Now, what were you doing in my cave?"

Laura scowled. "I've told this idiot," she said, pointing at Block, "a million times already. I was looking for my dog. Who are *you*?"

Clovis Monk ignored her question and continued his own interrogation. "Who showed you the way? Prince Paul?"

"No! No one did," Laura retaliated.

"Was it the prince's bodyguard?" Monk leant forward menacingly, watching for her reaction.

"No, it was not. And, anyway, how do you know about them?" she asked.

Monk gave a sinister laugh. "Because, little sprite, I make it my business to know. And little children are strictly forbidden to meddle in my business!"

"I wasn't meddling!" cried Laura in defiant exasperation. "And I want to go home now, please."

Monk shook his head slowly. "Knowing the secret of Voltan's statue? I think not, sweetie. You'll be our guest for a little while yet... Block, feed the girl."

And with that, Monk swept out of the room, followed closely by his own two bodyguards.

A few minutes later, Block came back in with a tray of food. "Supper," he said curtly, dumping the tray in front of her.

Laura, pushing the tray away and fixing Block with her most obnoxious glare, said crossly, "I don't want your horrible food, I want to go home. You have no right to keep me here!"

Block thrust the tray back at her. "Ungrateful little wretch! EAT!"

Laura reached forward meekly but at the last moment, twisted the glass of milk up with a deft flick and flung it into Block's face. She sprang towards the electronic door in a desperate bid to escape, but her way was instantly blocked by two guards. They picked her up, kicking and screaming, and plonked her quickly back into the chair. Block was apoplectic with anger. He pulled one of his gloves off and whipped it up as if about to strike her. His eyes were terrifying.

But Laura faced him bravely. "DON'T YOU DARE!" she shouted.

The firelight flickered on Ruby's tired face. She leant forward to warm her hands. "It's past midnight, Barney. Why isn't the Royal Guard here yet?"

Barney, slumping drowsily back in the armchair opposite, stiffened slightly. He fiddled nervously with a fringed cushion as he answered. "Well, um… uh… It takes time to organise a search party in countryside like this. Listen, Ruby, kids are survivors. Laura will turn up, I promise."

Ruby shook her head doubtfully. "I hope so, Barney, I really do. I feel so useless just sitting here." She stared anxiously into the crackling fire, hoping that the boys were asleep.

But upstairs in the boys' room, a huge and very hairy spider crept over Mike's bedclothes and down his pyjama leg. Pausing only briefly to sink its pincers into his foot, it climbed down the leg of the bed and scuttled off under the wardrobe. Mike tossed and turned fitfully.

"AAARGH!" he screamed suddenly, and sat bolt upright.

"Jeepers, Mike!" growled Jack sleepily, switching on the bedside lamp. "You all right?"

Mike smiled sheepishly. "Sorry, Jack. Dreamt I'd been bitten by a humungous spider!"

Paul, yawning widely, squirmed out of bed. "Since we're all awake," he said, plonking himself next to Mike, "what do you think of Barney's theory that Prince took Laura's ribbon into the cave?"

"No way," said Jack vehemently. "I think she must have been there."

Peggy poked her head round the bedroom door and, seeing them awake, shuffled in. "Couldn't sleep. I thought I heard wolves howling."

"Are there wolves, Paul?" asked Mike tremulously.

Paul nodded.

"No wonder Barney was so keen to get back before nightfall," Jack remarked.

"Pah! Barney!" hissed Paul dismissively.

Peggy changed the subject. "Why hasn't the Royal Guard arrived yet?"

Paul stood up. "I don't know. But I'm going to phone Dad to find out."

The door closed quietly behind him. Mike imagined the worst scenario. "Suppose they don't come. What then?"

Peggy ruffled his hair. "Don't be silly. Of course they'll come."

"But the wolves might've got her by then!" said Mike, suddenly frightened for his twin.

"Shut up, Mike, you misery!" said Jack.

Peggy clutched her dressing gown even more tightly round her. "I wish Dad were here. He'd know what to do."

Paul tiptoed back to the bedroom. Mike, Jack and Peggy turned to him expectantly. "The blasted phones aren't working," he said.

"Great! We still don't know when they're arriving, then," Peggy complained.

"Aargh!" Mike clutched his stomach. He suddenly felt distinctly queasy and light-headed. "Or even if—" he groaned.

"There's only one thing to do!" Jack sounded absolutely determined as he pulled his clothes on. "We have to go back to that cave!"

In answer, Paul reached for his clothes.

Mike groaned heavily and rolled back. "I feel s-o-o dizzy," he moaned.

Peggy felt his hot forehead. "Mike, you stay here and rest."

Mike shook his head and tried to sit up. He couldn't believe how weak he felt. "But I want to come—"

Peggy pulled the duvet up under his chin, then followed Paul and Jack out of the room. She turned to check on Mike as she closed the door.

He appeared to be fast asleep already. "You'll be OK. We'll find Laura for you. Don't worry," she whispered, and flew to her room to get dressed too.

The three children crept slowly down the stairs and into the sitting room. "Shhh!" Paul hastily put a finger to his lips.

A snort alerted Jack and Peggy to the danger. Barney had fallen asleep in the armchair and was snoring heavily. Jack waved them on towards the door, and with Prince on their heels, they crept past the big man and out into the night.

CHAPTER NINE

Ruby's eyes snapped open. Perhaps she'd imagined the noise. She slipped out of bed and tiptoed to the boys' room. Both Jack and Paul's beds were empty!

"Mike!… Mike!" she shook him awake.

"Wh-what?" said Mike drowsily.

"Where are the others?" Ruby prodded him.

"Gone to look for Laura," he murmured faintly.

"Oh, no!" Ruby sighed with exasperation.

"Ruby!" Mike cried pathetically as she left the room, but she didn't hear. She was too preoccupied thinking of the others wandering about in the dark forest. Mike dropped back onto the pillow in a dead faint.

She dressed quickly and hurried down to where Barney slept in the armchair. "Huh! Some bodyguard," she grumbled to herself as she failed to wake him. She braced herself, and went alone into the pitch black night.

Using only one of their torches, Peggy, Jack and Paul made their way into the dark recess of the cave. Prince bounded in ahead, barking excitedly. As they reached the statue and stood wondering what to do next, the dog snuffled round its base, yapping and whining.

Paul scratched his head. "There must be a clue here. Prince isn't so interested in it for no reason. Everybody take a section and we'll examine every square centimetre."

They spent some time going over each piece carefully, but nobody found anything.

"It looks like we've drawn a blank," said Jack at last in disappointment. "I've been over this part four times and all I've got to show for it is a dirty finger!" He showed the others his hand. "Look at this muck! It must have been there for years!"

"Ugh!" said Paul. "What on earth's that from?"

Jack grinned. "His ear!"

"It's gross!" said Paul. "My ear wasn't like that!"

"That's funny," puzzled Peggy. "Why should one ear be filthy and the other clean?"

Jack looked at her for a moment, then at the ear that Paul had been checking. He reached up and felt around.

"Ha! There's something here – it's like a little trigger." He strained with the effort of reaching so high. There was a click. "There!"

They all stepped back, gazing in

astonishment as the wings of the statue slid open. For a moment they were speechless. Then they stepped into the brightly lit tunnel beyond. No one noticed footsteps coming up behind them. They crept forward cautiously.

Peggy heard a noise and spun round, but it was too late. "Oh no! It's closing!" she cried.

On the cave side, Ruby rushed up to the statue just as its wings closed over the tunnel entrance.

"Peggy, Jack, Paul!" she pleaded. "Please, come back!" She thumped her fists uselessly against the cold, unyielding stone.

"Keep calm, keep calm," she told herself, trying desperately to think straight. At last it became clear what she had to do. "Barney! I have to get Barney."

Wet branches brushed against her face as she hurried through the unfamiliar woodland. "Please, please, PLEASE let this be the right way," Ruby muttered breathlessly. "Otherwise, I'll end up as some hungry wolf's breakfast."

In the distance, the headlights of a lorry swept through the darkness. "Saved! It must be the Royal Guard, at last." She sprinted towards it.

Thaddeus was down to his last coin. The others lay bent and discarded about his feet. He kissed the last one for luck and forced it under the lid of the crate. He gave an almighty heave and to his immense relief the lid lifted just enough for him to wedge his fingers into the gap. Finally, he managed to lever the whole thing up.

"Thad, you're a genius!" cried Charlotte. She stood up awkwardly, shaking and rubbing the numbness from her limbs.

The lorry suddenly lurched to a halt and a door slammed.

"Get down, quick!" warned Thaddeus and bundled her back into the crate.

"Are you serious?!" she said, resisting.

"Someone's coming, don't argue!" He dragged the lid back into place, and had just enough time to hide under a tarpaulin before the tailgate was lowered and a light shone in.

"OK, Ms Clancy, time for a little walk," sniggered one of the thugs as he hauled her out of the crate. "Come on, lady."

"You'll never get away with this!" warned Charlotte, struggling wildly. "Whoever you are, you're making one big mistake— Oi!... Ow!"

The guard grabbed her wrist and snapped a handcuff over it. He secured the other cuff to his own wrist.

"Where are we?" demanded Charlotte, staring at the six men in camouflage gear and balaclavas who were lined up in front of her, and then at the dark forest surrounding them.

"Shut up, lady, and wait quietly if you know what's good for you." The man known as Toad then directed his men, "OK, lads, let's unload this medical gear, sharpish."

Charlotte, terrified the men would discover Thaddeus under the tarpaulin, watched nervously as they unloaded the lorry.

Ruby, who was just about to burst into this scene, suddenly sensed there was something peculiar going on. She stopped and peered at the clearing from behind a tree, hardly believing what she saw. A woman was being frog-marched into the darkness behind a group of men dressed in camouflage gear.

"Am I dreaming, or is that Charlotte?" she whispered, closing her eyes for a second and giving her head a quick shake. When she opened them it was even more strange.

"Thaddeus! What on earth?" she gasped.

She saw him leap from the lorry as it moved away and run into the shadows beside the road. Just as Ruby was about to call to him, he raced off after Charlotte and her captors.

"Something very weird is going on here," she muttered under her breath. Now it was even more important that she get back to the lodge.

"No choice now. We must go on," said Paul, turning back from the closed door into the sloping tunnel ahead of them. After a moment's hesitation, Peggy and Jack followed.

"This is all man-made," said Jack, thumping the wall.

"Yes. And modern," agreed Peggy. "Nothing to do with Voltan."

They caught up with Paul. "Where do you think it leads?" asked Jack.

"Well," said Paul, thinking of their compass position, "if we keep on in this direction – the Secret Forest."

For a moment Peggy and Jack thought he was joking.

"Wh—? But surely… No… She wouldn't—" Jack spluttered incoherently.

But Peggy knew what he was trying to say. "Jack's right. She wouldn't have gone on her own. Someone must've taken her!"

"Shhh!" Jack suddenly grasped Peggy's arm. The three children froze in mid-step, and were horrified to hear the sound of rapidly advancing footsteps.

"Come on! This way. Quick!" Paul dived up some steps on their right.

Peggy and Jack didn't need any persuading. They leapt nimbly after him, followed by Prince. They skidded round the corner at the top and slammed themselves against the wall, holding their breath. Peggy slid to the corner and v-e-r-y slowly eased her head round. She gasped, and whipped it back. A man in camouflage uniform and wearing a balaclava was mounting the steps. Peggy screwed up her eyes and, pressing her body flat against the wall, prayed for a miracle.

CHAPTER TEN

Peggy held her breath as the steps came nearer and nearer – and then suddenly she heard a shout! Had she been seen? She heard a voice say, "Oi, Watson, come on. We've been recalled to Sector Seven. Move it!" The command seemed to come from the bottom of the steps.

"Coming, Sarge," the man she'd seen answered.

The three children listened as the sound of heavy feet clumped down the tunnel.

"Phew! That was close!" whispered Jack, letting out a huge breath.

"I really thought," hiccuped Peggy, giggling hysterically, "we were goners."

Her laughter was infectious. For a minute or two they fell about, chuckling helplessly, even though they knew they should be keeping as quiet as possible.

Finally they pulled themselves together and carried on up the tunnel, keeping their ears pricked for the slightest noise. The tunnel seemed to go on for miles; junctions and stairs led off in every direction, but Paul did his best to keep them going north.

At the top of a small flight of stairs, he

stopped abruptly. At the bottom, a black metal grille, cast in the shape of an intricate spider's web, barred their way.

"Wow!" said Jack. He felt a strange mixture of admiration and fear.

Paul loped down the steps two at a time and reached out his hand.

"DON'T TOUCH IT!" yelled Jack.

Paul leapt back, almost jumping out of his skin in surprise.

"It could be a trap!" Jack warned. He picked up a large pot that was lying nearby, and motioned Paul to stand back. He threw the pot at the metal web. A blinding flash and a shower of fizzing hot sparks exploded about them.

"Phew! It must be wired with zillions of volts!" said Jack, coughing.

"But we can't get through! We're stuck!" wailed Peggy.

They were all looking at one another, not sure what to do next, when Prince suddenly pricked up his ears and whined urgently. They followed the dog's gaze. The shadow of a man was emerging round the curve of the tunnel on the other side of the grille. Silently, Paul dragged his friends behind a stack of large tins. They crouched down, their breathing shallow and quiet, as they watched.

Another man dressed in camouflage gear ambled up to the grille. He tapped a security code into a panel on the wall, then wrenched open the middle section of the web. The pot lay buckled and melted at his feet. He looked slightly surprised but, after glancing briefly up the tunnel, he kicked it lazily to one side.

"What's he doing now?" whispered Peggy.

Paul leant out a little. "He seems to be tapping some sort of password into the security box on this side. Probably re-setting it," he whispered. "B-L-A-C-K, Black! Black something!"

The spider web clanged shut behind the man, and he disappeared back down the tunnel. When it seemed safe, the children tumbled out of their hiding place.

"Come on, let's try it!" said Jack.

They clustered round the security box and Jack said, "I saw a W, an I, and maybe an O."

"Window?" suggested Paul, uncertainly.

"Black Window?" said Peggy doubtfully. "That doesn't make sense." But she began to key it in.

"WIDOW!" yelped Paul. "Of course! Black Widow! The spider!"

As Peggy finished tapping in the words, the web gate swung open.

Jack and Peggy beamed at Paul.

"You deserve a medal, kid," said Jack, imitating Barney's accent.

Paul laughed and pushed him through the grille. "Let's find Laura first!"

"At last!" huffed Ruby.

Dawn was breaking as she threaded her way through the gardens to the lodge. Dew glistened on the bushes and made the lawn slippery beneath her feet. She burst through the front door – and collided with a woman dressed in traditional Baronian costume.

"Oof!" The woman reeled back as Ruby fell across the threshold into her arms.

"Ohh! Sorry!" Ruby gasped as she regained her balance. She looked curiously at the plump, rosy-cheeked woman whose flaxen hair was braided in an elaborate spiral over her ears. "Who are you?" she asked.

The woman smiled. "Frau Bauble, housekeeper of Killimooin Lodge."

Suddenly Ruby remembered her mission. "BARNEY! Where's Barney?" she yelled.

Frau Bauble stepped back in surprise and pointed to the living room.

Ruby skidded to a halt in front of the dead fire, and shook the sleeping man vigorously. "Barney! Wake up! Quickly!"

He awoke with a start and stared at her, completely bewildered.

Ruby blurted out, "The children! They've gone. They went back. Through the cave. The statue closed behind them. I couldn't open it. I saw Charlotte and Thaddeus by a lorry. Soldiers in balaclavas were unloading boxes. They're holding Charlotte prisoner." She stopped to draw breath, "Oh, Barney, it was horrible!" She sank in a weary heap at his feet.

For a moment Barney sat in stunned silence, trying to absorb everything she'd told him.

Frau Bauble came in and began to bring the dead fire back to life.

"Whoa, Ruby," said Barney. "Start at the beginning! Who's Charlotte?" he asked.

Ruby sighed. To explain everything now seemed a waste of precious time. "She's a friend of the children's father. They're both supposed to be on a book tour. Back in England!"

"Are you sure the men were holding her prisoner?"

"Yes, of course," said Ruby impatiently. "She was handcuffed to one of them."

"Oh," said Barney. He almost sounded disappointed. "OK, this is what we'll do. We'll wait here for the Royal Guard. Meanwhile, we'll get you to bed, and Frau Bauble will bring you up a pot of tea."

Frau Bauble paused in her efforts with the fire. "Tea!" she cried. "I told you we have no tea here! Bertieverst is what we drink. Baronian wonderdrink. Good for everything – headache, broken bones, stomach pain…"

Ruby paid no attention. "But the children, Barney!"

"They're going to be just fine," Barney soothed. "Leave it to me. I'll take care of everything."

Ruby was too exhausted to argue or protest when Barney took her by the elbow and guided her towards her room.

The guards, laden with boxes, tramped along a forest track with Charlotte handcuffed to the last man in the group. Thaddeus, darting from tree to tree in close pursuit, saw them disappear into a cave and followed them. He watched in amazement as the wings of Voltan slid open. The guards trooped through, shuffling sideways to make room for the boxes they were carrying. Charlotte, too, was hauled in as if she was another piece of baggage.

As the statue's wings began to close, Thaddeus leapt over to the tunnel entrance and just managed to slip through before the doors ground shut.

CHAPTER ELEVEN

Far ahead, Peggy, Paul and Jack were still making their way along the apparently never-ending tunnels.

"Is it my imagination, or is the air getting fresher?" Paul said, sniffing.

"I think you're right!" Peggy whispered excitedly. "I'm sure I can feel a draught!"

"We've walked at least four miles. I reckon we must have reached the other side of the mountain!" said Jack, beginning to run.

Prince barked as if in agreement, and they all sped after Jack. Sure enough, after only a minute or so the children arrived at the end of the tunnel and came out into the open.

"Cor!" gasped Jack in amazement.

They all looked round, astonished. Before them stretched a wonderfully lush valley, misty and steaming in the early morning light. Luxuriant plants of every conceivable kind, ferns, creepers, exotic lilies, trees laden with strange fruit, all were jumbled together beneath the delicate branches of sweetly scented Persian lilac trees. Somewhere in the distance they heard the sound of a fast-running river.

"We're in the Secret Forest!" cried Paul.

Jack stayed calm. He said sensibly, "Well, we can't hang around, there could be guards anywhere."

"Hey, look!" cried Peggy, pointing at something on the ground. "It's Laura's other ribbon!"

"That settles it," said Jack. "She *is* here. Where to now?"

"This looks like the most worn track," said Paul. "And Prince seems pretty keen to go that way. OK with you two?"

Peggy and Jack nodded, and they tramped off with renewed enthusiasm.

Clovis Monk strode into his security room, followed closely by an agitated Block.

"Who dares to invade my territory?" snarled Monk, flinging a guard away from his post at the video monitor. He leant heavily on the table and surveyed the video screens with their sweeping views of the forest above.

He whipped his head round and glared at Laura who was looking at one of the screens with a mixture of horror and relief. She shrank back from the man's wild, unblinking eyes. He really was mad! Suddenly, he grabbed her shoulders and leant over her, his nose almost touching hers.

"Why did you lie to me?" he demanded, his piercing eyes boring into her.

"I didn't!" protested Laura, struggling stoutly to loosen his hold on her.

"Liar! You told me no one else knew about the cave!"

"They don't!" she insisted.

"Then how do you explain THAT?" Monk whipped an arm away and pointed to one of the video screens. Peggy, Jack, Paul and Prince were running along a path, completely oblivious of the surveillance cameras tracking their every move.

"I-I-I don't know," stammered Laura lamely.

"Pah!" Monk released her and sprang back. "Block, you weasel, get up to the forest and bring them in!" He swung round to the panel of video screens. "I'll activate the trap in Sector Four. And Block—" He turned to his second-in-command, who was gripped in a particularly bad spasm of head jerks and lip twitching. "No mistakes!" Clovis Monk was smiling, but the threat contained in the two words was quite clear.

Block backed out of the room, flinching and sweating, and incoherently gabbling loyal obedience to his merciless master.

"Like rats in a trap, my dear," muttered Monk.

Laura watched the screen helplessly as the others ran unsuspectingly towards danger. Monk's finger was poised above the release key. There was nothing Laura could do to stop him.

"Ah ha!" Monk gloated, and tapped the key.

Instinctively, Laura cried out to warn the children, although of course they couldn't hear. She watched in horror as a heavy web-like cage plunged down from the canopy of trees. It crashed onto the ground, imprisoning the three children beneath it.

Monk threw back his head and roared with laughter. He turned to Laura and said nastily, "Isn't this fun, little girl?"

Laura gritted her teeth. "You haven't got them yet, you beast!"

Monk slapped the table, laughing horribly. "See for yourself, whipper-snapper. It won't be long before you're all my little lab rats!"

"It's no good!" cried Peggy, reeling back from the edge of the trap. "It's too heavy. Unless—Maybe Prince could help?"

"Good thinking!" said Jack, abandoning his attempt to pull the bars apart. He called the dog over and pointed.

"Prince! Fetch that stick. Prince – the stick."

The dog obediently ran over to a thick branch

that had broken off a tree when the cage had crashed down.

"That's it! Pick it up, pick it up. Come on, boy."

Peggy and Paul joined in. "Good boy. Yes! Bring it here! Here, Prince!"

The dog managed to drag the branch to just within reach of Jack's hands. The children whooped jubilantly.

"Well done, Prince!" praised Peggy, stroking his ears through the bars.

"Out of the way, Peg. I'm going to pull it through," said Jack.

Paul found a large rock in the ground and dug it out with his heel. "Here you are! Use this to rest the branch on. Let's see if we can lever up the cage," he said, pushing the rock hard against the metal base.

"OK, you two," said Jack, forcing one end of the branch under the cage. "Grab the end and push down as hard as you can."

The three children used all their strength, and slowly, very slowly, they felt the cage begin to lift. Jack kicked the rock forward to support it.

"A little more!" he puffed. "That's it! Hold it!" There was just enough space for him to slide under. "OK, Paul next."

The cage was resting precariously on the

branch, which was beginning to break under the strain. Paul and Jack gripped hold of the cage to take some of the weight.

"OK, Peggy, crawl out, quick!"

Peggy didn't need to be told twice. She was out before Jack had finished his sentence. Prince leapt around them excitedly and Jack and Paul both whistled with relief as the cage crashed to the ground.

"Phew! That was a close shave. We'd better get moving before whoever set the trap comes to inspect their catch," said Jack.

Prince began barking frantically. Jack looked at him curiously. "Why's he barking again? He's been making that racket ever since we got here."

Prince's gaze was focused on the trees above them. Jack looked up too and his eyes widened. He pointed to something attached to a tree.

"Oh, no! A camera! No wonder we were caught so easily."

Peggy and Paul followed the direction of his finger.

"And there's another one!" Peggy pointed as the other camera turned slowly in their direction.

They all spun round as a twig cracked behind them.

"Someone's coming! Hurry! We have to get

off the path before they see us!" whispered Jack.

The children and Prince threw themselves into the undergrowth.

CHAPTER TWELVE

Monk leant back in his chair as the children disappeared off every video screen. "Mmm, they show considerable initiative," he muttered.

"That's because they're cleverer than you think!" Laura's delighted voice startled Monk.

"Is that so?" His eyes glittered with a fury that frightened Laura. "Well, when you and your friends all learn the value of obedience, you'll be worthy citizens of the New Era."

Laura looked puzzled. "New Era? What do you mean?"

"The Era of Clovis Monk! Master of the World!"

Laura shrank back in horror. He must be mad! No one who wasn't mad would have such an incredible idea.

Moments later, Monk snapped back to reality. "Activate cameras in Sector Seven!" he ordered.

The guard at his side obediently tapped a key on the computer.

Suddenly, a mobile phone trilled in Monk's pocket. He snatched it out and spoke to Block, who had just appeared on one of the screens accompanied by a platoon of guards. They were standing by the empty cage.

"Sector Seven, Block! They're heading this way!" Monk boomed as he swung round to watch the children's progress on the next screen. He clicked off the phone, and sat back to calculate the expected time of re-capture.

"This is impossible," cried Peggy. "We'll have to avoid the cameras or we'll be caught again!" She bent over to catch her breath as the others pushed their way through the undergrowth to join her.

"But how can we?" said Jack, panting.

Then Paul had a brainwave. "Surely the cameras are all linked by a cable? If we can find it, we can dodge them before we're spotted!"

Their eyes lit up and they began to scour the ground.

"There!" cried Peggy, indicating a bit of cable showing through the leaves. High above them in a tree, a camera silently scanned the area. "Quick, hide!" she yelled. "It's turning this way!"

Just in the nick of time, they all huddled together behind an enormous tree and the camera panned across an apparently child-free landscape. Peggy peered round the trunk.

"OK. It's turned in the opposite direction now. Let's go."

They followed the thick black cable for some distance.

"OK, same again," said Peggy, pointing up at the next camera.

Several times they avoided the eyes of the surveillance cameras and were able to hurry undetected through the forest.

"Oof!" Paul suddenly tripped over an unexpected secondary cable, and landed face down on the peaty ground. The cable filtered from beneath his nose not to another camera but to an electrical junction box a few feet away.

"Hey!" he yelled excitedly. "I think I've found the control unit for all the cameras!" He crawled over and wrenched open the lid. He leant in and pointed at the main wire. "If I disconnect this—" he began, and pulled firmly.

"YES!" Jack and Peggy cheered. "All the cameras have stopped moving!"

Paul waggled the disconnected cable in the air in triumph. Then, after a moment's thought, he said, "This is fine for now, but they probably have some kind of back-up system. We'll still have to keep out of sight of the cameras in case they get them working again." The others nodded, and they set off on the path once more, keeping a wary eye out for any pursuers.

*

Frustrated, Monk banged his fist on the table. No matter what command he punched into the computer, the video screens remained blank.

"See! What did I tell you?" said Laura, grinning.

Monk turned his blazing eyes upon her. "If you had any idea what's in store for you, little girl, you wouldn't dream of being so cocky!"

He whipped out his phone. "Block! What do you mean, no sign of them? I will not tolerate failure, Block. Do you understand?"

Laura stifled a giggle, which made Monk hiss at her, "Wipe that smile off your face, missy, before I do it for you!"

He turned to scream down the phone at Block, who was babbling fearfully at the other end.

"Request further sighting, Master."

"Shut up, you fool!" roared Monk. "And LISTEN! Get the men to form a protective barrier round the whole base. The intruders must not, I repeat, MUST NOT be permitted to breach our security any further. IS THAT CLEAR?"

"Why do I have to be handcuffed?" complained Charlotte loudly, as the guard wrenched her forward. Her wrists were already red and sore.

"Where on earth do you think I'm going to run to?" she asked as they trudged on through the Secret Forest.

The guard ignored her.

"Don't you guys ever say anything?" Charlotte flicked her head from side to side, trying to assess her chances of escape. Out of the corner of her eye she saw a bush move, and she twisted round to see properly.

"Oh!" Charlotte involuntarily let out a small gasp as Thaddeus popped his head up and gave her a thumbs-up sign.

The guard turned round to see what she was up to but Charlotte gave him an innocent smile and rubbed her wrist. He tugged at the handcuffs unsympathetically and she winced with pain.

"You're all such robots. Don't any of you have a mind of your own?" she railed, trying to get some kind of response from them.

A sudden high-pitched, leering laugh from further away made her turn round.

"Well, well. The award-winning journalist! So nice to see you up and about!" It was Block and his men. He walked towards her, a cruel smile on his face. "I fear there will be no awards for you on this trip!" he sniggered nastily.

"Tell your gorillas to take the handcuffs off me!" demanded Charlotte, straining forward.

Block laughed. "What an extraordinary creature you are! Completely in the master's power and yet still you think you can dictate to us!"

Charlotte sneered. "Master! Is that what you call your sleazeball boss these days?"

Block frowned and twitched, a vein in his cheek throbbing.

"You're pushing your luck, Clancy."

"*I'm* pushing my luck! You've committed theft, assault and abduction—"

Block clamped his hand over her mouth to silence her.

"You've put our project behind five years with your meddling!" he hissed at her.

Suddenly, he wheeled round. A movement in the bushes behind her had caught his attention. Signalling a guard to accompany him, Block stepped off the track to go and investigate.

Charlotte had to think fast for a way to distract him from discovering Thaddeus.

"Hey! Do they still call you 'Twitchy'?" she called.

Block stopped dead in his tracks and spun round, instantly forgetting what he'd been going to do.

"WHAT?" he spat, his nostrils flaring. "*What* did you call me?"

Charlotte grinned. She had him now.

"Remember? The nickname the papers gave you during the trial?"

Block's eyes blinked uncontrollably, his lip curled, and his neck stiffened. He was livid with rage. For a moment he couldn't even speak, his throat felt so tight.

"No one, but *no one*, calls me that. Understand?" he squawked.

Charlotte laughed. "You mean none of these guys ever calls you TWITCHY? I bet they want to," she taunted him.

Block's face went into another unnatural movement. He turned to the commander and screamed hysterically, "Gag her if she says it again! Now, get moving!"

CHAPTER THIRTEEN

"Shhh! A guard!" Jack put a finger to his lips and they all sank back into the undergrowth.

Peggy's fingers grazed against something cold and hard jutting up out of the ground. She gave the guard a few minutes to get out of earshot, then beckoned to the others to come and look. Once she'd swept away the leaves, they could see an opening about a metre square, covered by a metal grille.

"I think it's a well or shaft of some kind," whispered Peggy, lifting the grille. They all peered into it.

"It only goes down about two metres, then it seems to turn at a right angle," Paul whispered.

"Of course!" exclaimed Jack. "How stupid of me!"

The others looked at him in surprise. What did he mean?

"That's the reason you can't see anything from the air! It's all underground!" Jack explained.

Peggy and Paul still looked puzzled.

Jack pointed to the opening. "This is a ventilation shaft!" he explained.

Prince gave a low whine.

"There's a guard heading this way. Quick! Get in!" Jack hissed. "Lucky there's a ladder."

The children clambered into the shaft and pulled down the grille.

"Oh no! It won't quite close," said Peggy, desperately trying to pull the grille back into place before the guard spotted them. But it wouldn't budge, and Prince was still standing there, not wanting to leave the children.

"Go walkies, Prince! Go walkies!" Peggy hissed. The dog looked mournfully through the grille at her and then obediently ran off.

It worked. Just before the guard reached the shaft, he heard the dog moving through bushes some way from the track. He immediately changed direction to investigate.

Not daring to move, the three children huddled together on the ladder inside the shaft. They looked upwards and listened for any sound that might indicate the guard's return.

"I think it's safe to go up now," said Paul, after what seemed like hours.

"UP?" said Jack in amazement. "We've got to go on!"

Paul stared at him. "What? Down there?" he asked, pointing into the gloom that stretched below them.

"Of course," said Jack. "It's our best bet for

finding Laura, don't you think?"

"You're right," Peggy agreed emphatically.

Paul sighed and let Jack squeeze past him. He crawled forward on his hands and knees, and the others crawled round the bend after him.

Prince led the guard on a merry chase through the forest, twisting and turning until the man was well and truly lost. The dog then made his way silently back to the ventilation shaft. He looked through the grille just in time to see Peggy at the bottom as she disappeared from sight round the bend. He whined softly and pawed noisily at the metal grille. Peggy's voice floated up to him.

"Shhh, Prince. Sit! We'll be back soon."

Prince slumped down next to the grille. If he couldn't go with them, he could at least keep watch!

Thaddeus was slowly and quietly approaching the camouflaged entrance to Monk's base. Only a few moments before, he'd seen Block and the guards march Charlotte through its steel door, which they had opened by sliding a card through a box in the wall. He took out the card he'd found in the guard's wallet back at the warehouse in England, and swiped the card through the security panel as he'd seen Block do. Nothing happened. He tried it the other way round. Yes, that was it! The door slid open.

Looking round to check that he was not being watched, Thaddeus slipped into the passageway. It sloped sharply downwards into the bowels of the earth. In the distance he could hear the regimented sound of heavy boots stomping along the corridor. He started to run down the passage.

Deeper in the hidden complex, the three children passed behind a whirring extractor fan and crawled down into the next section of the shaft.

Jack stopped abruptly and held up his hand.

"Listen! Voices!" he said.

Paul gripped Jack's ankle and waggled it in warning.

"If we can hear them, they can hear us," he whispered.

Thinking it was lucky they were all wearing trainers and wouldn't have been making too much noise, Jack nodded. He inched forward to peer through a square grille. He pressed his face to the wire mesh, and gasped.

Pacing agitatedly to and fro in the room below was a long-haired man in a white suit. His eyes were fixed on a wall of blank video monitors, and he was shouting at a guard sitting at a computer keyboard.

"Try Sector Five!... Sector Four!... Right, that does it. Get out there and fix those cameras!" he ordered, pushing the guard off his chair.

Laura was tied to a chair beside the table facing the ventilation grille.

"Thank goodness," breathed Jack, relieved to have found her at last.

He motioned to Paul and Peggy to keep quiet as they moved forward to look through the grille. They were about to try and attract Laura's attention when Block twitched and spluttered his way into the room, simpering and genuflecting before his boss.

"M-Master— eeek!"

Block found himself suddenly pinned against the wall and staring into Monk's mad eyes.

"Three children and a dog, Block. And you, you simple-minded idiot, let them escape!"

"You'll never catch them. They're far too clever for you!" cried Laura, wriggling about in her seat.

Monk released Block, who slid to the floor like a rag doll.

"Silence!" he roared, giving Laura's chair a vicious kick.

Laura managed to steady herself and yelled

back at Monk, "Don't shout at me, you horrible man!"

Block crawled his way up the wall and, humbling himself before Monk, whined for forgiveness.

"We will find them, Master. I'm truly, truly sorry."

Monk's anger subsided and in a relatively calm voice he asked, "Where's the prisoner?"

Block brightened somewhat. "Sh-she's being held, M-master – the Clancy woman – in the Venom Sector."

CHAPTER FOURTEEN

While Block was grovelling to his master and stammering out the details of Charlotte's capture, Jack scratched lightly against the grille and whispered, "Laura!"

She frowned and leant forward slightly, staring at the wall opposite. She spied Jack's outline and let out a startled "Oh!" Quickly glancing at Monk and Block, she saw that luckily they were far too involved in their own wrangling to have heard anything.

Hardly daring to breathe, Laura turned away but flicked her eyes up at the ventilation grille. Yes! They were there! She could just make out Jack's familiar green eyes and wide grin. Her eyes lit up and she found it difficult not to let out a whoop of delight.

Monk turned away from Block and poked the remaining guard, "You're wasting your time here. Get out into the forest and join the search for the rest of those pesky children. Come with me, Block. And bring the girl with you."

Block untied Laura and yanked her roughly out of the chair.

"You're coming with us, little miss," he said dragging her along behind Monk.

Laura gave Jack a despairing look over her shoulder as the electronic door closed behind her. Peggy watched carefully as Block passed his security card through the control panel to open the door.

Jack pushed the grille and it swung open easily on hinges. He jumped through, dropped onto a filing cabinet, and from there sprang nimbly to the floor. Paul and Peggy followed, shutting the grille quietly behind them.

Jack tiptoed to the door and peered out. "I'll keep watch. You two see if you can find any useful clues about what's going on here."

Peggy scanned the blank video monitors and the clutter of medical equipment on the table. A security card emblazoned with a spider emblem caught her eye and she scooped it up to examine it more closely.

"Someone's coming!" warned Jack.

The three children squeezed behind a filing cabinet in the corner of the room. The door slid open and, without them seeing him, Thaddeus looked round the room. Charlotte obviously wasn't in there so he quietly withdrew to continue his search.

"Phew! That was too close for comfort!" gasped Peggy as they tumbled out of their hiding place. "Just imagine if we'd been caught by those horrible men!"

They crept to the door and peered through its glass panel.

"All clear!" whispered Jack.

Peggy tried swiping the card through the security panel – and it worked! The door opened and they hurried out into the corridor.

Back at the lodge, Frau Bauble bustled into the boys' bedroom with a broom and spotted Mike in the bed.

"Oops! Sorry, my little potato! I thought all the children had gone!"

Mike lay comatose and silent as Frau Bauble pulled the duvet up under his chin and peered at him curiously.

"You asleep, little one?" she asked, feeling his forehead. It was ice-cold. She looked anxious and shook his shoulders gently, but he did not stir.

Ruby appeared in the doorway, yawning widely and stretching.

"Morning, Frau Bauble. Mike—" She suddenly noticed the look of concern on the housekeeper's face and hurried to Mike's bedside. "What's wrong? Mike?!... Mike!"

He groaned and his eyelids fluttered.

"That's it, Mike, wake up, come on!" Ruby

felt his brow again. "You're freezing!"

Mike pushed her hand away weakly and moaned, "I'm boiling, Rube!"

"Most mysterious!" said Frau Bauble, shaking her head.

"I think I'll call the doctor. It looks pretty serious to me," said Ruby, unconsciously biting her lip.

Frau Bauble threw up her hands in horror.

"No. No doctor! The bertieverst!" she insisted.

Ruby stared at her, wide-eyed. "I beg your pardon?"

The housekeeper swirled round to leave the room. "The bertieverst. It will cure the little potato. It cures everything!" she cried gaily. "It is medicine from wild mountain flowers. I go pick some now!"

Ruby turned back to Mike and plumped up his pillows before running downstairs to find Barney. She heard him talking as she burst into the room.

"Yes, I understand. I'll do it immediately. Of course you can rely on me." Barney put down the phone and began to pace the room. He flinched at Ruby's unexpected entrance.

She smiled at him. "Was that the Royal Guard?" she asked eagerly.

For a moment he looked caught out, and then he answered, "Er, no, it was the... er... the... er... King! Yes, the King. He... ah... appreciates what you did last night."

Ruby shrugged her shoulders. "I didn't do anything."

Barney put his arm round her shoulder. "Well, sure you did, Ruby. How are you feeling this morning?"

Ruby laughed. "Terrible! But listen, Barney, where are the Royal Guard?"

"They're here, they're here. They're setting up a command post in the... um... In the barn."

Ruby's eyes lit up.

"I'll take you over there," said Barney, leading her out onto the porch and towards the barn. "Now, are you sure you told me everything?" he asked.

"Yes!" said Ruby indignantly. "I didn't imagine it, if that's what you're implying."

The barn seemed awfully quiet.

"Where did you say the Royal Guard were?" she asked.

"They must be searching the grounds. The commander is using the barn as an office. After you," said Barney, graciously stepping aside for her.

Ruby looked around, puzzled. "Is this some

kind of joke, Barney?" she asked. The only thing in the barn was a cream-coloured nanny goat. It bleated at her.

"I'm afraid not!" he answered and, in one deft movement, slipped a thick rope over her shoulders and pulled a loop tightly round her arms, pinning them to her side.

"Hey!" shouted Ruby, trying to steady herself. "What's going on?"

"Don't struggle. You'll only make it harder for both of us," said Barney miserably.

Ruby stared at him, hardly able to believe what was happening. Suddenly, it all became clear. "Oh no! You're in on this too, aren't you?" she cried. Her eyes widened with horror, then flamed with anger.

"Where are the children?" she demanded. "What's happened to them?" She bent double, ran towards him and rammed her head into his stomach.

Barney picked her up and plonked her down on a bale of straw. He tied another rope round her ankles, then drew out a piece of fabric. Before she could say another word, he had tied it tightly across her mouth.

"I'm sorry, Ruby, truly I am." He gave her an apologetic smile and left the barn, bolting the door securely behind him.

CHAPTER FIFTEEN

As Barney trudged back into the lodge his mobile phone trilled. He let it ring, half believing he had the strength of will not to answer. But it was no good. Within a minute he had lifted it to his ear.

"Hello?" He yanked his hair at the roots, angry at himself for being so weak. "No, not yet. I was just about to," he muttered into the receiver. He didn't like what he was hearing at the other end of the phone at all. "Yes, I understand the penalty for failure."

He flicked the phone shut and took a deep, steadying breath. He pulled his knapsack towards him and, scowling thoughtfully, drew out a small glass box. He stared at the venomous spider inside it and began to sweat.

"I'm so, so sorry, Ruby. I don't want to do this to you, but I have no choice."

"Help! Help! Hel-l-l-lp!" Ruby's pleas were heard by no one but the goat. It nuzzled her hands and began nibbling at the rope round her wrists.

"Oh, you angel! Come on, darling, a little more! Try this little knot." Ruby spluttered the words through the gag and as she attempted to shift her body closer to the creature she toppled face down into a pile of straw.

But the goat chewed on happily. Ruby's shoulders heaved and she began to chuckle.

"Rescued by a goat! No one will ever believe it!"

At last she could flex her arms, and soon she felt the rope give way entirely. She wrenched the gag from her mouth and sighed with relief.

"Gee, thanks, pal," she said gratefully, giving the goat a hearty scratch under the chin. "I hope I can do the same for you one day!"

She spotted a saw hanging on a nail and hastily pulled herself up and jumped towards it. She hacked at the bonds round her ankles until she was free.

"Right, let's see what we have here," she said, surveying the barn. She made a beeline for a magnificent old motorbike. Next to it she found a dusty helmet and a pair of goggles.

"Perfect!" She pulled them on, and wheeled the motorbike into the centre of the barn.

Barney was plodding back towards the barn with a heavy heart. He reached the door and took another deep breath. He held up the glass box and stared at the poisonous spider. He flipped up the lid. No! He couldn't, he wouldn't do it! He bent down and tipped the spider onto a rock. "You may not make it in this climate, pal, but you'll have to take your chances. What the—?"

The cough and splutter of an engine roared from within the barn. Barney bounded to the door and pulled back the bolt. He wrenched it open.

"No, Ruby!"

She thundered past him onto the forest track. Barney ran after her, yelling, "Ruby! I wasn't going to hurt you! Honestly! Stop! I have to talk to you!"

In the Venom Sector of his secret laboratories, Monk cradled a large glass case containing at least four spiders.

"So," he said, slowly raising his eyes to meet hers. "Charlotte Clancy, we meet again. How does it feel to be on the receiving end for once?" He snorted with amusement.

"Cut the cackle, Clovis. Why have you kidnapped me? You're taking a big risk if you're just out for revenge," Charlotte challenged, folding her arms defiantly.

Monk laughed.

"Do you know what this is?" he asked, pulling a small glass phial from his pocket and letting it swing between his thumb and forefinger. Inside it, the pale green liquid lapped gently up and down.

"Aftershave?" Charlotte suggested flippantly. "Bat saliva?"

"Oh, my goodness, how very witty in adversity," he mocked, leaning forward menacingly. "No, my dear Ms Clancy, this is a very special spider poison. It induces paralysis, followed by death in—"

"Forty-eight hours." Charlotte finished the sentence.

"Hmmm. As well informed as ever!" Monk sneered. "But this poison is different." He pulled out an identical phial from his other pocket. "The spider produces its own antidote. All I need now is a final test."

Thaddeus's life depended on Charlotte getting hold of the antidote in Monk's hands, but she forced herself to sound calm as she asked, "What's the point of it?"

Monk smiled condescendingly. "The point, my dear, is that by taking it you become both alive and dead at the same time. No breathing, no heartbeat, but still alive. For years, if necessary!"

Monk put the phials down on the table so as to admire them.

"But why?" persisted Charlotte.

"Oh," said Monk in amusement, "didn't I mention that? Allow me…"

He tapped into his computer and gestured towards the screen.

"A map of Baronia? So?" Charlotte said, curious.

"You see the forest river? Well, when my lovely little concoction comes into contact with water it replicates itself. I need only put a litre in that river, and in time it will multiply and spread across the entire world!" Monk shivered with pleasure.

"But you'll just end up with millions of living dead. What good will that be to you?" Charlotte asked, staring at him in horror.

"Only I shall have the power to reactivate them. They will be my people. I will RULE THE WORLD! And you—" He leant forward and stroked her cheek. "You shall be the first!"

Charlotte shrank back from his horrible hands.

Monk pushed a button on his desk and spoke into a microphone. "Bring our other visitor in, Block. Ms Clancy might like to entertain her."

The door opened with its electronic swish, and Laura came in with Block. "Charlotte!" she cried, pulling away from Block's restraining grasp and flinging herself at her father's friend.

"Laura! What are you doing here?" gasped Charlotte, clutching her tightly.

"LAURA!" thundered Monk. "You mean you two know each other? Is there no end to this conspiracy against me?"

"Don't be absurd! There is no conspiracy. She's just a child – let her go!" Charlotte demanded.

But Monk was too furious to think rationally. "Tie them up, Block. Then come to me at the pod. It's time!" cried Monk and swept out of the room.

Block and the guard tied the protesting Charlotte and Laura up and hurried after Monk.

"So," said Charlotte, when they were alone. "Are the others here?"

Laura nodded. "Yes, but Monk doesn't know."

"Right," sighed Charlotte, shuffling her chair over to the table. "We'll have to find them. And we'll need to get those two phials, and find your dad, too."

"Dad! Is *he* here?" Laura asked, astonished.

Charlotte looked at her, wondering where to start, but there wasn't time. "Never mind for now. Let's just concentrate on getting out of here." She leant sideways and stretched her hands towards an empty glass flask.

"Got it!" She grasped the flask firmly and smashed it against the side of the table. The base splintered and showered around her feet. She scrunched her chair over the shards to reach Laura, and began sawing at the rope round her wrists with the sharp edge.

"Yes! You've done it!" whispered Laura triumphantly.

Charlotte was breathless. "OK, Laura, you do mine now. Then we can cut our legs free."

CHAPTER SIXTEEN

Again, the familiar sense of weakness was coming over Thaddeus, but he knew he had to find Charlotte. He staggered against a door and, breathing heavily, managed to swipe his stolen security card through the panel. The door slid open and Thaddeus stumbled in. A hospital theatre trolley stood against the far wall, draped in a pale green sheet. Attached at one end was a cylinder marked ANAESTHETIC. It had a face mask draped across its nozzle. Other cylinders lined the opposite wall. Thaddeus's vision began to blur and he sank to his knees. Through the foggy haze that seemed to have filled his head, he was aware of voices coming nearer.

"Have you completed all the measurements, Block?"

Thaddeus forced himself across the slippery floor, and clawed himself up onto the lower shelf of the trolley. With his last ounce of energy he drew the sheet neatly back into place. He lay down, willing himself, unsuccessfully, to ward off the encroaching blackness.

The door slid open.

"Yes, Master. She will require five litres of life-suspension gas," Block was saying as he trotted along like an obedient dog beside Clovis Monk.

"Excellent. Finish your security checks, and then get the woman."

"Yes, Master!" Block summoned two guards and ordered them to follow him. "Bring that trolley!" he commanded.

Thaddeus was only vaguely aware of a swaying sensation as the trolley was wheeled down the corridor. His last thought as he drifted into unconsciousness was that staying so still may at least save him from being discovered. He heard the faraway sound of a door sliding open, and then nothing.

Charlotte and Laura sawed through the bonds on their legs with the broken bottle.

"Right," said Charlotte. "Ready?"

"Yes," replied Laura, rubbing her wrists.

For a moment, Charlotte looked at the two bottles Monk had left on the table then picked them both up and together she and Laura made for the door.

"How do we get out of here?" she asked.

Laura looked at the door blankly. She had no idea. "Is there a button you can push, or something?" she asked.

Before Charlotte had a chance to reply the

door swished open and Block came in with two guards and the trolley. For a second he looked taken aback as he saw the two prisoners untied and ready to go, but then pulled himself together.

"Hhhmph!" he cackled. "Not your day is it, Clancy?"

Charlotte and Laura backed away from the door, and Charlotte pushed Laura protectively behind her. "Don't hurt her! Just leave her alone, I'll do anything you want."

Block grimaced. "How very considerate of you," he sneered, suddenly lunging at her. He held her hands tightly behind her back and pressed a mask over her face. There was a loud hiss as anaesthetic flowed into the connecting tube. Charlotte's startled eyes slowly drooped, and her body slumped into Block's arms.

"NO!" cried Laura, punching Block as he loaded Charlotte on top of the trolley.

He shoved her aside and pushed one of the guards towards her. "Tie the little pest up again!" he ordered.

Grabbing the trolley handle, Block wheeled Charlotte's motionless body out into the corridor.

Jack poked his head round the corner. He stared

in disbelief as a small group of men came out of a door and made their way down the opposite corridor pushing a trolley covered with a pale green sheet. He leant back against the wall.

"I must be going mad!" he whispered.

"Why?" Peggy asked.

"I'm sure I just saw Charlotte!" Jack told them.

"Who?" Paul was astonished.

"She was on a hospital trolley."

Peggy shook her head in disbelief. "That's impossible! She's on tour with Dad."

Jack thought for a moment. "No, I'm absolutely positive it was her. Come on, let's have a look in the room they came out of."

He and the others hurried down the corridor. Jack gently pushed the door ajar and peered round it. He couldn't believe his eyes!

"Laura!" He yelped and burst into the room. So this was where she'd been taken to.

"Jack!" Laura was delighted to see him.

"Are you all right?" he said, bending down to untie the rope round her wrists.

"Yes, but they've got Charlotte." She wriggled her hands free and stood up. Monk's handkerchief was on the table. She picked it up and wound it round her right wrist, which was bleeding a little from the rope.

"I *knew* it was her! How did she get here?" Jack asked.

"There's no time to explain. But Dad's here too."

"WHAT?" The others all looked astounded.

"He was following Charlotte and the men who caught her," she said. "But she doesn't know where he is now, and neither do I."

Jack scratched his head. All this was so confusing. "What on earth's going on, Laura?" he asked.

"That man you saw, the one in a white suit – that's Clovis Monk. I think he's mad. He's made a poison, and I think he's going to give it to Charlotte. We've got to rescue her!"

"Hey, look at this!" said Peggy, tapping away at the computer Monk had been using. She'd keyed in everything she could think of to try to find out what was going on in this mysterious underground set-up, and now something very interesting scrolled up on the screen.

The children crowded round her and watched as a succession of photographs flashed across the screen.

"Who are they?" Paul asked.

Peggy explained: "Agents linked to Monk's organisation. See, each has a number." She pointed to the screen.

"There are hundreds of them!" exclaimed Jack.

Peggy looked serious. "Yep, at least one from every country... I think he wants to rule the world!"

Laura tugged at her shoulder urgently. "Come on, Peg, we've got to find Charlotte before it's too late!"

"Hang on. Just let me check Baronia... Here we are... Oh no!"

The children stared in dismay as a familiar face stared out at them.

CHAPTER SEVENTEEN

"Barney!" Paul slapped his forehead. He'd always felt there was something fishy about that secret serviceman!

Jack pulled Paul away from the computer. "Forget about it. Right now, our first priority is to find Charlotte and Dad! Come on! Peggy, where's the card?"

Peggy swiped the security card she'd found earlier through the code panel. The door swished open and the children saw another corridor. "The trouble is," Peggy whispered as they crept along, "even if we do find her, we can't possibly fight all the guards. They're everywhere."

Jack put his arm round her shoulders. "It'll just need a bit of cunning, Peg. We've beaten them so far, haven't we?"

Peggy had to admit he was right, but it didn't make her feel any better.

Laura grabbed their coats and pointed to a wide glass window in the wall opposite. The children all ducked down and squirmed their way across the floor until they were crouching beneath it. Slowly, each of them lifted their heads until they could just see over the ledge.

"Charlotte!" they all gasped. But Charlotte

was surrounded by guards, and even Jack knew that there was nothing they could do to rescue her. They listened instead to what Monk was saying.

"Careful! We don't want to damage our first human experiment." He was watching over the transfer of Charlotte's limp body from the hospital trolley and into a pod-like container.

"There! Good!" said Monk. "Now, before we administer the poison—" he pressed a button, and silently the glass lid of the capsule closed over Charlotte. "And so the process begins! Load the life-preserving gas!" he commanded.

Block turned a switch and slowly the pod began to fill with a white mist.

Monk checked a reading on one of the monitoring units. "Very good. Keep the temperature constant. We don't want our first specimen to perish, do we?" His eyes glowed with madness.

"He's such a horrible man!" whispered Laura. "We *must* do something. We must create a diversion before they give her the poison, or—" Her eyes opened wide in alarm and she dropped to the floor. "Uh-oh! He's seen us! RUN!"

Monk screamed frenzied orders: "After them! Seize them! They will be my next disciples! Don't let them get away!"

Block and a number of guards ran from the room in pursuit of the children. Monk swirled about angrily, issuing orders in every direction, and then addressing two guards in particular. "YOU, stay here and watch the woman!" He pulled back two of the men to stand guard over Charlotte. "It's imperative that we keep the temperature at a steady 40°. Monitor it constantly!"

Thaddeus surfaced slowly into what, at first, seemed to be a pale green tent. He blinked bleary eyes, and felt the strength gradually returning to his leaden limbs. The rhythmic whir and bleep of medical equipment filled the air. "Am I in hospital?" he wondered vaguely.

Then he remembered! He eased aside a flap of the sheet and peered out. Two men in camouflage gear were standing with their backs to him but there didn't seem to be anyone else in the room. Thaddeus stretched up to reach the two anaesthetic masks that were dangling from the trolley handle. He then began the difficult task of climbing stealthily from the trolley shelf without the guards hearing. At last he was crouching just behind them. In one fluid movement he jumped up, clamped a mask over each of their faces, and blasted them with a good whiff of sleeping gas.

Almost immediately, the guards slumped unconscious to the floor.

"Charlotte!" Thaddeus rushed over to the pod and in a panic began tearing at the lid. "How does this blasted thing open?" He examined all the buttons and switches, trying to discover which would do it. Then once again a terrible weakness engulfed him.

"Oh no! Not now! Not so soooon…" His vision blurred, his legs buckled and he fainted once more.

The temperature gauge was flashing a warning.

TEMPERATURE ABOVE ACCEPTABLE LEVEL.
DANGER! REDUCE TEMPERATURE IMMEDIATELY OR ABORT ANIMATION SUSPENSION.
REPEAT. TEMPERATURE ABOVE ACCEPTABLE LEVEL, AND RISING. ABORT SUSPENSION IMMEDIATELY! DANGER! DANGER! DANGER!

Barney stopped running and inhaled great gulping breaths of air. Just then, on a mountain road well below him, Ruby roared round a hairpin bend and came into view at the bottom of a steep slope. Barney saw a jeep bouncing along at high speed towards her.

"Oh no! Ruby! Stop!" he screamed and pounded down the rough track in the same direction. But Ruby didn't hear either the jeep, or Barney, because of the old-fashioned helmet she was wearing. Nor did she *see* the jeep, until the last minute.

The jeep screeched to a stop in front of her, blocking her route. Ruby skidded to a halt too and lifted her goggles, ready to give the driver a piece of her mind.

"Why don't you look where you're go—"

Suddenly, Ruby realised this was no accident. There was something very menacing in the way the guard was striding towards her. She began to protest.

"Look, I don't know who you are, or what you want, but you've got the wrong person here," she said, pointing to herself, and smiling wanly at the guard. "I'm just on holiday. Do you know what I mean?" She flipped her leg over the bike and backed away.

The guard's only reply was to brandish a truncheon.

"Oh no, you don't!" cried Ruby, frantically looking about for something she could use as a weapon.

Just then, a small black object hurtled past

from behind her. It struck the guard squarely on the head and he dropped to the ground, unconscious.

Ruby grabbed his truncheon as it rolled away, and spun round, her knees bent in a position of self-defence.

"Barney!" She was so surprised to see him that she straightened up, but dropped down again instantly and held the truncheon threateningly in front of her. "Don't you come near me, you... you... obnoxious cowboy!"

"Aw, Ruby!" he pleaded, holding out his hands to show he was unarmed, "Please let me talk to you." He took a tentative step forward.

"KEEP YOUR DISTANCE!" Ruby warned him and shook the truncheon savagely.

CHAPTER EIGHTEEN

Barney stopped and held up his hands in a gesture of peace. "OK, but Ruby, listen, I'm sorry. I didn't want to do it, but, well—" It all came tumbling out. "A few years ago, when I was a government agent, I sold some secrets to a guy called Clovis Monk and he—" Barney swallowed with embarrassment. "He's been blackmailing me ever since."

Ruby shifted from one leg to another. "So," she said scathingly, "you've been working with him all along, huh?"

"No! Well, yes. But it shouldn't have been a problem. The King wanted me to keep the kids safe, and Monk wanted me to keep people off the mountain and away from the cave. You see, by doing one job, I could do the other and satisfy both parties. But it all went wrong when Laura disappeared." He gave her a pleading look.

Ruby plumped her hands on her hips. "And that's why you didn't want to search up there? And you never called the Royal Guard, right?"

Barney nodded. "Right. I disconnected the phones, too, so no one could check. Ruby, I honestly thought it would all blow over."

Ruby wasn't finished with him yet. "What

about tying me up like a trussed chicken?"

He gave her a thin, apologetic smile. "They wanted me to kill you – with a poisonous spider."

"Charming!" huffed Ruby.

"But I couldn't do it!" Barney said quickly. He shook his head. "I've been foolish and I've been weak and cowardly, but no matter what they do to me, I would never hurt you. And that's the truth."

The pair of them stood staring at one another – Barney pleadingly, Ruby full of suspicion.

Suddenly, the silence was interrupted by the loud ringing of Barney's mobile phone. It had landed at Ruby's feet after Barney had thrown it at the guard. Ruby scooped it up and threw it over to him. She still wasn't sure if she should trust him.

"Hello?" said Barney uncertainly. "No, I haven't." He grew bolder. "And I don't intend to. I don't care any more. Do what you like! Your days are numbered, Monk. I'm off to get the Royal Guard. Don't wait up!" And he lifted an arm and flung the phone as far away from him as he could into the depths of the forest.

"Well, that was bright," sighed Ruby. "We could've used it to phone the King, and saved ourselves a journey!"

Barney looked mortified as he realised how stupid he'd been, but Ruby shrugged her shoulders and tossed the truncheon away. She clambered onto the motorbike, and said, "Hop on, mister! I'm going that way myself!"

They grinned at one another. Picking up the guard's crash helmet from the jeep, Barney swept it before him in a mock bow and said, "Ma'am, don't mind if I do!" and leapt up behind her to ride pillion.

Pandemonium was breaking out everywhere in Monk's underground lair. Alarm sirens wailed along all the tunnels and there was a thunder of running boots as the guards split up into search parties to look for the children.

Monk, who had just been speaking to Barney, smashed his mobile phone furiously to the floor. "Block! BLOCK!" he shouted.

Block stumbled up the corridor towards his master and sank to his knees in front of him. Monk began to scream at him.

"That feeble-minded milksop Barney Stokes has gone renegade! You must get rid of him immediately!"

Poor Block was so agitated he couldn't speak. He opened his mouth to answer, but his head was jerking and his nose and lips were twitching so badly that he couldn't get out a single word.

"JUST DO IT!" screamed Monk and pushed Block out of the way as he stormed past.

DANGER! DANGER!
TEMPERATURE CRITICAL. ABORT SUSPENSION.
DANGER! DANGER! DANGER!
TEMPERATURE CRITICAL. ABORT SUSPENSION.

In the Venom Sector, slumped beside the pod, Thaddeus coughed and stirred deliriously.

"Something's burning," he murmured. "Turn the oven off!"

The smell was acrid and he coughed again. He sat up, feeling foggily light-headed. There was a painful ringing sound in his ears. He rubbed his eyes and shook his head. The bodies of the guards he'd knocked out lay sprawled next to him. Thaddeus looked puzzled, and then his memory began to seep back.

"What the—? Oh, jeepers! Charlotte!" He pulled his leaden body up to the pod. Steam was pouring into the capsule and leaking out into the room. The CRITICAL WARNING sign flashed again and a blue light began to blink.

"No time to waste!" Thaddeus coughed as he

studied the control panel of the capsule again. There were so many buttons and switches! He hurriedly pressed each of them in turn, until, at last, the lid of the pod slid open. A great plume of steam rose from it, forcing Thaddeus to hang back for a moment. He took a deep breath and, narrowing his eyes against the stinging mist, leant into the capsule. He dragged Charlotte's body out of the death trap and placed her gently on the floor. He turned to the two unconscious guards and began pulling off their uniforms.

"We'll never get out of here, even if we do find Dad and Charlotte! It's like a maze!" cried Laura, stumbling after the others. "Oooomph!" She crashed into Jack, who'd come to an abrupt halt when he saw what was in front of him.

"Turn back!" he shouted. "More guards ahead!"

The children turned and hurried back down the corridor, hotly pursued by the guards.

"They're catching up!" yelled Paul, looking over his shoulder. They skidded round a corner and practically fell over Prince, who'd been tearing down the corridor towards them. The dog barked in rapturous delight and then bounded back the way he'd come, turning every few minutes to make sure they were following.

"What's he doing here?" cried Laura.

"I don't know!" answered Jack. "But let's follow him anyway! We've nothing to lose."

Thaddeus dressed Charlotte in camouflage gear and pulled a balaclava over her head. He was sure that this was the only way to get out of the underground bunker – they'd have to bluff their way past the guards. He pulled on a matching outfit himself, swung Charlotte's arm over his shoulder and gripped her round the waist. Then he hauled her up and dragged her out of the room.

Charlotte's head hung limply on her chest and in his weakened state it took an enormous effort for Thaddeus to support her. He could hear the pounding feet of guards racing down the corridor outside, obviously pursuing someone. But it was too late to turn back. He stepped out with brazen audacity and was almost knocked over as a group of similarly dressed men swerved around them.

"Sorry, mate!" said the leader of the pack. "Fugitives just passed this way!"

Hurrying off, Thaddeus nodded towards his limp companion and in a gruff voice said, "He's taken a spider bite – needs fresh air."

Without a second glance and hardly slowing

their pace, the other guards resumed their chase.

At long last, Thaddeus staggered up the stairs to the exit. It felt as though he was carrying a hippopotamus, not a person. A guard stepped forward, barring his way. Thaddeus thought fast.

"Get down there, quick! There's an emergency!" he yelled. He was so convincing, the guard jumped to attention before flying past him down the steps. Thank heavens all the guards were wearing balaclavas – no one had asked him any questions at all! Thaddeus sighed with relief and for a moment rested against the outer door. He flung his balaclava away and scrabbled around in his pocket for the spider security card.

When the door slid open, he heaved Charlotte back up over his shoulder and carried her shakily towards an overgrown trail through the forest. He knew he had to get her as far away as possible before he blacked out again. He forced himself onwards with faltering steps.

Finally, his strength drained away and he sank to the ground. Gently, he laid Charlotte beside him and took off her balaclava.

"Charlie!" he begged, clutching and rubbing her cold hand. "Charlie, please wake up!"

CHAPTER NINETEEN

Monk burst into the Venom Sector, his eyes blazing. He kicked at the bodies of the two guards who were slumped on the floor and dressed only in their underwear and socks. The pod which had contained Charlotte was empty, and Block was shaking with fear beside him.

"Master—" Block's snivelling tone added fuel to the madman's fury.

"THE WOMAN! FIND HER!" he shouted, twisting Block's ear.

"Yes, Master. I-I just think you should know—" He screwed up his eyes, trying to find the courage to speak. "The little girl is missing." He cringed away from the expected beating. "And we can't find the children."

"WHAT?" Monk shrieked in fury.

Block's mouth twitched again. "We've searched everywhere, Master. They're not here." His voice was squeaky with terror.

"Then how did they get out?" demanded Monk, pacing the floor.

"I–I don't know, Master."

"You idiot! You let a bunch of kids outwit you!" Monk slammed his fist down on the blackened pod. Suddenly, he looked up at the ventilation grille. He stroked his beard as he realised what must have happened. "There's one way they could have got out."

Block followed his master's stare. "Ah! Of course! The grille!" he realised, and his head twitched in another nervous spasm.

"You know what to do, Block?" Monk questioned, quietly for once.

"Yes, Master," Block replied.

"You hero, Prince!" praised Jack as the dog led them safely into a ventilation shaft. They scrambled along it as fast as they could.

Laura was almost crying. "Poor Charlotte. It's horrible!" she whimpered.

"And what if that horrible man's caught Dad as well?" said Jack anxiously.

"He hasn't caught Dad!" cried Peggy.

"How do you know?" queried Jack.

"Of course he hasn't," maintained Laura stoutly. "We've got to find him."

"If only we knew where he was," Peggy said.

Paul sniffed loudly. "What's that weird smell?" he asked.

Wisps of pink smoke began to waft about them.

"I can't see properly!" complained Laura.

They all began to cough as the smoke grew

more dense.

"Ooh! It stings," cried Peggy, rubbing her eyes.

Jack's eyes closed. Prince barked and tugged at his sleeve. They were all suddenly feeling an overwhelming desire to sleep.

"Prince, get help! Fetch Ruby! Fetch Dad!" cried Laura.

One by one, each of the children stopped coughing and slumped unconscious against the hard metal surface. Prince scrambled along the shaft to an exit and burst out into the sunlit forest.

Charlotte pressed a hand against her thumping head. When she finally managed to open her eyes, she blinked in astonishment. She dug her elbows into the ground and hitched herself up a little.

"What—?" she muttered in surprise at the camouflage uniform she was wearing. "How on earth—?"

Then she spotted Thaddeus, out cold, propped against a nearby tree stump. Charlotte looked at her watch and, closing her eyes, frantically worked out the number of hours that had passed since the spider had bitten him. Her eyes snapped open. Forty-eight! She lifted the camouflage jacket and dug her hand into her own pocket beneath it. The two glass phials clinked and she drew them out with relief. Then she hesitated. They looked identical. Which was the poison and which the antidote?

"Oh, no!" she cried in frustration, looking from one to the other in panic. Then she brightened. It was a risk but she had no choice. She cradled Thaddeus's head in her arms and carefully lifted one of the phials to his mouth...

To her enormous relief, he opened his eyes within seconds.

"Charlotte!" He coughed and sat up.

"You OK, Thad?" she asked, looking at him anxiously.

He frowned. "I don't know. Am I? I have a terrible taste in my mouth," he said, coughing again.

Charlotte laughed. "Well, you should watch what you drink. Especially spider antidotes!"

She chinked the two empty bottles together. "Meet poison and antidote."

Thaddeus felt the stubble on his face. "How did you know which to give me?" he asked, rising unsteadily to his feet.

"I didn't. I gave you both. I figured the antidote would cancel out the poison either way!" she said, giving him a hand.

"Brilliant, Sherlock!" he laughed. "Come on, let's get out of here."

Charlotte caught his arm. "Thad, there's something you should know. The children are in Monk's headquarters."

Thaddeus stopped dead in his tracks. "*What*? How did they get there?"

"It's a long story," said Charlotte.

"If that lunatic has harmed a hair on their heads, so help me I'll—" He strode off through the trees.

Charlotte raced after him and blocked his path. "I presume you have a plan, Thaddeus? Or are you just intending to barge in there and get caught?" she asked.

"They're my children!" cried Thaddeus.

"Exactly! So for goodness' sake, give some thought to what you're going to do!"

Thaddeus pushed past her, too worried to take in the sense of what she was saying, and ran down the forest track. Charlotte had no choice but to go after him.

"Damn! We're lost! How can we be lost? I'm sure I didn't carry you this far from the entrance," shouted Thaddeus after a few minutes.

"Calm down, Thad," Charlotte gasped, trying to catch her breath. "Look, this stream must lead to the river, and—"

Thaddeus held up his hand to silence her. "Someone's coming!"

They dived behind a tree and peered cautiously round its trunk. Prince bounded up to them, barking joyfully. Enormously relieved, Thaddeus bent down and gave him a hearty rub. He held the dog's face in his hands and looked him in the eye.

"Prince, do you know where they are? Jack? Laura? Peggy?"

Prince barked excitedly in reply.

"He does! Prince, seek Laura! Seek Laura!"

Thaddeus and Charlotte raced after the dog as he scurried away through the undergrowth.

CHAPTER TWENTY

Ruby roared into the city at top speed. Barney was clutching her round the waist and hanging on for dear life.

At last they saw the palace and Ruby revved the old motorbike's engine even higher. At the sound of their approach, a guard stepped sedately out of the sentry box and held up his hand. But nothing was going to stop Ruby now and she ploughed straight for him. His eyes grew wider and wider. No one had ever before questioned his authority. Only when they were almost upon him did he manage to shake himself out of his stupefied trance and leap out of harm's way.

Ruby and Barney skidded to a halt in front of the palace, abandoned the bike, and rushed up the steps to the grand entrance. Scattering a host of astonished sentries aside, they ran determinedly through the arched doorway and on into the great hall. The alarmed King stood up and faced them as they burst into the respectful silence of his throne room.

"What is the meaning of this outrage?" he demanded.

Ruby struggled away from the sentries as

they caught up with her. "Just back off, will you, I've got to talk to the King!" She sounded so ferocious that they did fall back a little.

"I'm sorry, your Majesty," she gasped, "but it can't wait. The children are missing in the Secret Forest!"

The King looked startled. "What? How?"

Barney stepped forward and, with equal urgency, confirmed what Ruby had said. "It's true, sir. There's an evil man at work there. You've got to send in the Royal Guard before it's too late!"

"I trust you're feeling fully recovered," Monk asked the children coldly. "I insisted they only give you a mild dose."

Paul shook his fist at him. "You won't get away with this, you evil creep!"

Monk gave him a patronising pat on the head. "You've done well to evade me, little ones. You'll be worthy citizens of the New Era." As if drawn by a magnet, he slid over to the numerous glass display cases laid out on the table. He stroked each case in turn, crooning at the hundreds of spiders crawling about inside them.

"So, my darlings, soon your precious poison will help me rule the world!" His voice was soft and his eyes shone with joy. "When my guards release the formula into the reservoirs of all the great cities, the whole world will be paralysed." His eyes moistened with emotion. "Most people I shall leave to rot, but a few – who've proved their worthiness – I shall allow to live."

"You're mad!" cried Peggy. "It'll never work!"

Monk laughed maniacally. "You think not, eh? Then see for yourself!" He lifted one of the cases.

"NO!" shrieked Peggy. She took a deep breath, opened her mouth and screamed so shrilly that at times it seemed almost inaudible.

"Silence!" roared Monk, protectively encircling the cases with his arms.

Laura, who had been watching Peggy in great consternation, suddenly realised what her sister was trying to do. She took a huge lungful of air and began screaming too.

Holding their hands over their ears, the children increased the pitch and intensity until the sound was almost unbearable.

Monk pressed himself desperately against the cases. By turns, he cursed the girls in demented rage, and sought to reassure his darlings with the smoothest of tones and caresses. But the prolonged onslaught of high-pitched sound waves began to have the effect Peggy hoped for.

The cases began to quiver under the onslaught, and the spiders jumped and shuddered inside them.

"STOP IT! STOP IT! You're disturbing my precious friends!" Monk could see what was likely to happen. Tears began to stream down his stricken face. The guards seemed rooted to the spot, their hands clamped over their ears, their teeth clenched in agony.

The screaming became ever louder. The whole room seemed to shake in the grip of the terrible noise. The children clutched one another and backed towards the door. Jack grabbed a folded piece of tarpaulin and flung it round them. Peggy and Laura gasped in a quick breath and screamed one final deafening note.

There was an ear-splitting sound of splintering glass. And the next second every case in the room exploded under the intense pressure. Spiders and shards of glass catapulted into the air at great speed, and rained down in a brutal hailstorm on Monk and his guards. There was total chaos.

"Come on!" cried Jack, shaking off their protective tarpaulin. "Let's get out of here!"

The children dashed towards the door, scrunching over glass and spiders alike.

"You'll pay for this!" screamed Monk. He

grasped at Jack and pulled him back towards him.

Jack struggled to escape but he was no match for the madman's strength. Monk gripped Jack's hair and dragged him further back into the room.

"You'll pay for it NOW!" Monk raged – and then abruptly let Jack go. He'd caught sight of the enormous spider that was limping weakly up his arm.

"Oh, my babies!" moaned Monk, sinking slowly to the floor. "My poor, darling babies."

Jack raced out of the door and caught up with the others as they hurried along corridor after corridor, narrowly evading the guards, who seemed to be pursuing them from all directions.

"Oh no, a dead end!" cried Peggy, sliding round a corner and coming to an abrupt halt outside a storeroom. They could hear the sound of heavy feet pounding along the passage.

"Try the security card, quick!" said Jack.

Peggy whipped it out and flicked it through the control panel.

"Yes!" The door slid open and they tumbled in.

"Right! Barricade, everyone!" yelled Jack.

Hardly daring to breathe, the children heaved a large table and a filing cabinet against the door. But they were not left alone for more than a few moments – one of the guards had spotted where they'd gone, and was soon attacking the door with a sledgehammer.

Then came Monk's voice. "Resistance is futile! Give up now. You might as well get it over with!"

"Oh, this is hopeless!" cried Laura. "We're trapped whatever we do!"

CHAPTER TWENTY-ONE

"They haven't got us yet!" said Jack, sounding more confident than he felt. Laura looked thoroughly miserable as she plonked herself heavily against a pile of long blue cylinders. Peggy looked at what she was sitting on.

"And they're not going to!" she cried excitedly.

"What?" said Paul in surprise. He couldn't see how they could possibly escape.

Peggy grinned and, moving Laura aside, pointed to the cylinders. In bold lettering, they were marked: ANAESTHETIC. An array of masks lined the shelf above them.

"Get it?" said Peggy.

Another sledgehammer blow slammed into the metal. "I demand you open this door," ordered Monk. To his astonishment, a few minutes later he heard the children give up.

"All right. We'll let you in," called Peggy.

There was a scraping sound as the children hauled back the furniture. The door flew open.

"Sensible girl. Wh—? What pathetic little game is this?"

The room was pitch black and silent. Monk pushed Block and the guards in before him and flicked the light switch.

"NOW!" cried Paul.

Jack slammed the door shut and the villains found themselves surrounded. Each of the children was wearing a gas mask, and on Paul's command, they opened up all the taps on the cylinders of anaesthetic. The air in the room was instantly dense with the same red smoke that, on Monk's instructions, had been poured into the ventilation system when the children were in there. The guards coughed and wheezed, and then fell to the floor in an unconscious heap.

The children hurried to the door, but started back in horror when a loud thud sounded against it.

"Hey! Open up! It's me!" came an anxious voice.

"Dad!" They all cried with relief.

Paul wrenched open the door and they all stumbled out into his arms, slamming the door shut behind them. Prince pranced wildly about their feet, licking everyone and barking.

"Charlie, you're alive!" cried Peggy, tearing off her mask, and hugging Charlotte.

"Yep. Thanks to your dad!" Charlotte beamed at Thaddeus.

They started along the corridor, Thaddeus with his arms round two children on each side.

"Well, it doesn't look as if *you* needed my help!" he laughed.

Jack jigged up and down. "We used anaesthetic! It was Laura's idea." He felt justifiably triumphant.

"Hey, where's Mike?" asked Thaddeus, suddenly noticing his youngest son's absence.

"He wasn't feeling well. He stayed at the lodge," explained Laura. She dug her hands into her pocket and something silky touched her fingertips. It was Monk's handkerchief that she'd tied round her wrist when it was bleeding. She gasped. "Monk wasn't there!" she cried out.

The others looked at her in surprise.

"What do you mean? Not where?" asked Thaddeus.

"In the heap. In the excitement I didn't really notice, but now I come to think of it, I'm sure he wasn't in the storeroom when we left."

"You're right!" said Paul. "I know! I bet he escaped through one of the ventilation shafts!"

They all looked at one another in horror.

"He'll have gone to the river!" Laura said, biting her lip.

"Of course!" cried Jack. "He said he was going to poison the world from there!"

"Well, what are we waiting for? Come on!" urged Thaddeus, breaking into a run.

When they reached the exit, Laura pressed the handkerchief to Prince's nose. "Seek, Prince. Seek Monk."

The dog snuffled about the ground for a moment and then gave a sharp yap.

"He's picked up the scent! Good dog, Prince!" said Thaddeus, and they all hurried into the forest after him.

"There he is!" cried Peggy.

Monk was staggering as fast as he could towards the river. He was obviously still suffering from the after-effects of the anaesthetic and wasn't making good time. They rapidly caught up with him, and positioned themselves as a barrier between him and the rushing water.

"Don't be a fool, Monk. It's all over," said Thaddeus.

Monk swayed unsteadily on his feet and swept his arm through the air.

"Get back!" His voice was laboured and thick. He pulled a glass tube from his pocket and brandished it in front of them. It was filled with a pale green liquid.

"Yes. All over – for YOU!" he shrieked, reeling forward and yelling, "Let the New Era begin!" He hurled the tube high above the river.

Thaddeus, Charlotte and the children watched, speechless, as it curved over their heads. It seemed to twist and turn in awful slow motion as it spun through the air. It started its inevitable descent. There was no way anybody could stop it. The world was doomed!

Clink!... SPLOOSH!

Prince launched himself into the air at lightning speed and caught the tube deftly in his jaws. Fountains of water erupted above him as he sank from sight.

Everyone gasped with amazement, then fear.

Monk strained forward, waiting anxiously for the dog to surface.

Suddenly, Prince emerged, shaking water off his long hair. The tube, still in his mouth, was intact and glistening with water.

"Brilliant! Wow!" the four children chorused.

"He did it!" sighed Laura, clutching Thaddeus by the hand as the whole party leapt about cheering and whooping with delight.

Monk sank to the ground in demented agony.

CHAPTER TWENTY-TWO

"Well," said Thaddeus as they walked in a happy gaggle towards Killimooin Lodge, "it's a good thing the Royal Guard finally turned up. I don't think Monk and Block will get out of your father's dungeon in a hurry, Paul!"

"Never, if I can help it!" the young prince laughed.

Ruby put her arm round his shoulders. "I'm so glad the King said he would pardon Barney. He isn't really a bad man, just misguided."

"What an adventure!" sighed Laura.

"And poor old Mike missed it all!" cried Peggy, running up to the veranda.

"What's wrong with him, anyway?" asked Charlotte.

"He felt dizzy and sick," said Laura.

Ruby nodded. "Yes. He had a bit of a fainting spell."

Thaddeus stopped in his tracks. "What?"

Charlotte put a hand on his arm to steady him. "Have you seen any spiders round here, Ruby?" she asked urgently.

"Yes. A huge one up in my bedroom. You should have seen the si—"

Thaddeus and Charlotte sprinted into the

lodge without another word. Ruby and the children were completely puzzled. It was not as if Mike was dying. They looked at one another blankly for a moment and then hurried in after them.

Thaddeus and Charlotte rushed into Mike's room. He was lying quite still, his eyes closed. Charlotte pointed to his ankle. There were the clear puncture marks of a Maluku Devil Spider!

All the colour drained from Thaddeus's face. "Do you have the antidote?" he demanded.

Charlotte shook her head. "No, I gave it all to you, Thad!"

Thaddeus turned hopelessly back to Mike.

"Dad, what's wrong?" cried Peggy as she and the others appeared in the doorway.

Before he could answer, Frau Bauble bustled in past them. "Hello, hello! How's my little potato?" she clucked.

"Call the hospital, quickly!" shouted Charlotte.

"What's up?" said Mike sleepily. "Who's ill?"

Thaddeus and Charlotte swung round in astonishment. Mike was sitting up, looking very perky, as if he had just woken from a very refreshing sleep.

Thaddeus felt Mike's forehead and peered into his eyes.

"How do you feel?" he asked.

Mike grinned. "Great!"

Thaddeus couldn't believe it. "But how—?"

"It's the bertieverst!" explained Frau Bauble, as though it were the most obvious thing in the world.

"The... er... what?" stammered Thaddeus.

Prince Paul interjected. "Bertieverst! The Baronian magic potion!"

Mike grimaced. "It tastes worse than Ruby's soup, Dad!"

"Oh no! Not that bad!" groaned Jack.

"Hey!" said Ruby, laughing.

Frau Bauble clapped her hands together proudly. "Maybe so, but it cures everything. Even the spider bites, my little potato!"